Books by Diana Palmer

Silhouette Romance

Silhouette Special Edition

Silhouette Desire

To Ruth in Sydney, Australia

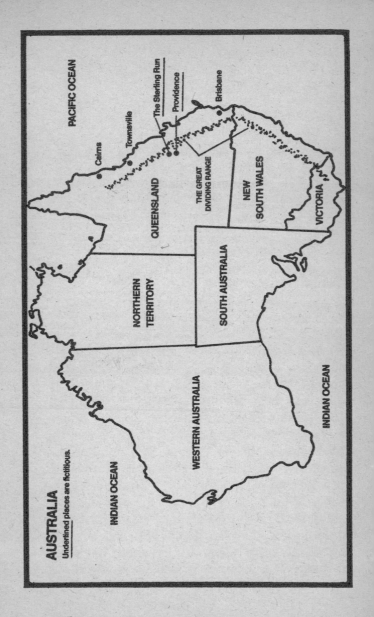

AUSTRALIA
Underlined places are fictitious.

PACIFIC OCEAN

The Sterling Run
Providence
Brisbane

Cairns
Townsville

QUEENSLAND

THE GREAT
DIVIDING RANGE

NEW
SOUTH WALES

VICTORIA

NORTHERN
TERRITORY

SOUTH AUSTRALIA

WESTERN AUSTRALIA

INDIAN OCEAN

INDIAN OCEAN

Chapter One

The airport at Brisbane was crowded, just as Priscilla Johnson had expected. She'd left Australia a college girl, but her college days were now over. With graduation had come the slow, sad process of severing friendships in Honolulu and leaving Aunt Margaret's house, where she'd lived for five years. Now the future held a teaching career in Providence, a small town northwest of Brisbane across the rain forests of Queensland's Great Dividing Range.

She looked around excitedly for her father and mother, and smiled when she remembered how happy they'd been about her plans to teach in Australia. It had been touch and go, that decision. If Ronald George hadn't been coming here to teach himself, if he hadn't prodded her . . .

She shifted from one navy pump-clad foot to the other. Her blonde hair curled in short wisps around her delicate oval face with its wide green eyes and creamy complexion. Those eyes were quiet and confident and just a little mischievous even now as she approached her twenty-fourth birthday. She walked with a fluid, easy grace, a result of the charm school classes her aunt Margaret had paid for. And in her white linen suit and powder blue blouse and navy accessories, she was a far cry from the teenager who'd left Australia so reluctantly five years ago to go away to college in Hawaii.

Priscilla shivered a little. Here in Australia it was spring in late September, not autumn as it had been in Hawaii. Her seasons, like her senses, were turned upside down. She'd had only two years in Queensland, after all, before college began. Her parents had left their native Alabama after Adam Johnson had applied and been accepted for a teaching position in Providence. He'd liked the idea of working in a small school mainly populated by children from three large cattle and sheep stations in the fairly remote area. Renée, Priscilla's mother, had been equally enthusiastic about the move. Neither of them had close family anymore: there were no other people to consider. All three of them had an adventurous streak. So they'd packed up and moved to Australia. And so far none of them had regretted it. Except perhaps Priscilla.

She wondered how it would be to see him again. Inevitably she would. Providence and the surrounding country were sparsely inhabited, and everyone met sooner or later in the small town to buy supplies or go to church or just socialize. Her thin brows drew together in a worried frown. It had been five years. She was a different woman now. Besides, Ronald would be settling in soon, and she'd have someone to keep her mind off Jonathan Sterling.

John. It was impossible not to remember. Her green eyes grew hard, and she clutched her purse and carry-on bag until her knuckles went white. Her memory hadn't dulled. Neither had the pain.

She was tired. It had been a long flight, and despite the fact that most of her luggage had already been shipped over and she was only carrying a small bag, she wished her parents would appear. She wanted to get back to the small cottage where they lived, on the fringe of the mammoth cattle and sheep station known as the Sterling Run.

Her eyes wandered quickly around the crowded terminal, but before they could sweep past the front entrance, she saw a broad-shouldered man standing a full head above the crowd of travelers. Her heart slammed up against her throat, and she began to tremble. Perhaps she was mistaken! But no, his hair was light brown with bleached blond streaks all through it, thick and slightly shaggy in back, and straight. He was wearing an old tweed jacket with gray slacks and dingo boots, but even so he drew women's eyes as he strode through the crowd.

His pale blue eyes swept the travelers, and he scowled. His dimpled chin jutted pugnaciously; his firm mouth was set in a thin line. There were new wrinkles in that strong craggy face. Her eyes searched him like hands, looking for breaks.

He hadn't recognized her yet. Of course not, she reminded herself. She'd left here a long-legged gangly teenager with waist-length blonde hair and ill-fitting clothing. Now she was much more poised, a sophisticated woman with confident carriage and designer clothing. No, she thought bitterly, he wouldn't recognize her.

She picked up her carryall and went toward him gracefully. He glanced at her with faint appreciation before his eyes took up their search of the crowd again. It wasn't until she stopped just in front of him that he looked at her once more, and his eyebrows shot together with the shock of recognition that flared in his pale eyes.

"Priss?" he asked uncertainly, his eyes

punctuating his astonishment as they ran up and down her slender body.

"Yes, it's me," she said with a cool smile. "How are you, John?"

He didn't reply. If anything, he grew colder as he registered the new poise about her.

"I'm waiting for my parents," she continued. "Have you seen them?"

"I've come to fetch you on their behalf," he said coldly, in the familiar Australian drawl that she remembered so well. He towered over her, big and broad and sexy as he pulled a cigarette from his pocket and lit it, while his eyes followed the lift of her eyebrows. "They had to attend some sort of luncheon in Providence."

She shifted her weight slightly, hoping her parents hadn't arranged this whole thing out of misguided affection. "Oh."

"You don't have to spell it out," he said on a cold laugh. "I'm no more anxious for your company than you are for mine, I assure you. But I could hardly refuse when I was asked. And I did have to be in town today."

"I can always ride in the trunk, if you like," she returned with an arctic smile.

He didn't even bother to reply. He picked up her carryall and turned, starting toward the front of the terminal and leaving her to follow or not as she chose.

She had to practically run to keep up with him, and that made her angry. "Still the master of the situation, I see," she threw at him. "You haven't changed at all!"

He didn't turn his head or break stride. His face only grew harder. "Well, you have," he replied. He glanced sideways, and there were angry glints in his eyes. "I didn't recognize you."

Once a remark like that would have devastated her. But over the bitter years she'd learned control. She'd learned to hide her heart. So she only smiled carelessly. "It's been five years, after all, John," she reminded him, and had to bite her tongue to keep from asking if he liked the change.

"That suit must have cost a mint," he remarked.

She laughed up at him. "It did. Surely you didn't expect a ragged urchin, John?" she chided. Her eyes wandered over his own garb. "Odd, I remember you as being more immaculate."

His eyes darkened dangerously. "I'm a working man."

Her nose wrinkled. "Yes, I remember," she said. "Sheep and cattle and dust."

"There was a time when you didn't mind," he reminded her and abruptly turned out of the terminal, his voice sharper than she ever remembered hearing it.

Yes, she thought, there had been a time when she wouldn't have minded if he was caked in dust or covered with bits of wool. Her eyes closed for an instant on a wave of pain and humiliation and grief that almost buckled her knees. But she had to be strong. She had to remember more than just the beginning. She had to remember the end.

Her head lifted, and her own eyes darkened. That would do it, she told herself. Remembering the end would do it every time.

"How's the college boy?" he queried as he unlocked the door of his late-model white Ford and put her inside.

"Ronald George, you mean?" she asked.

He went around and got in himself and stretched his long powerful legs under the dash as he started the car. "Yes, Ronald George," he replied, making an insult of the name.

"He'll be here Monday," she told him, delivering the blow with cold satisfaction.

His eyes narrowed on her face. "What?"

"He's going to teach with Dad and me in Providence," she said. "He's looking forward to the experience of small-town life."

"Why here?" he asked narrowly.

"Why not?" she said flippantly and smiled at him. "Ronald and I have a special relationship." Which was true. They were the very best of friends.

His eyes swept over her, and he turned back to ease the car out of the terminal parking lot with a low humorless laugh. "Well, I'm not all that surprised," he said. "You were ripe for an affair when you left Australia."

She flushed, turning her head out the window. She didn't like remembering how he knew that. "How's your mother?" she asked.

"She's doing very well, thanks," he replied after a minute. He put out his finished cigarette and lit another as they drove through Brisbane. "She tells me she loves California."

"California?" she asked. "Isn't she living with you anymore? I know she had a sister in California, but . . ."

"She lives with her sister now."

He didn't offer more conversation, so she busied herself staring around at the landscape. Brisbane seemed as foreign as it had that first day when she'd come here with her parents from Alabama. She sighed, smiling at the tall palms and golden wattle and royal poinciana trees towering over the subtropical plants that reminded her of Hawaii. Brisbane was a city of almost a million people, with gardens and parks, museums and galleries. With the Gold Coast and the Great Barrier Reef nearby, it drew constant hordes of tourists. It was a city that Priss often had wished she'd had time to tour.

She would have loved to see Early Lane, which re-created a pioneer town—including an aboriginal dwelling called a *gunyah*. John

Sterling had two aboriginal stockmen, named Big Ben and Little Ben, because they were father and son. Big Ben had tried unsuccessfully for days to try to teach Priss how to throw a boomerang. She smiled a little ruefully. Another place she had always wanted to see was New Farm Park, on the Brisbane River east of the city. Over 12,000 rose bushes were in wild bloom there from September through November, and the scent and color were reputed to be breathtaking. If she'd been with her parents, she would have asked them to drive there, even though it was out of the way. But she couldn't ask John.

He headed out of Brisbane, and she settled back in her seat, watching the countryside change. Outside the city, in the Great Dividing Range, was tropical rain forest. She could see copious orchids and scores of lorikeets and parakeets and other tropical birds flying from tree to tree. There were pythons in that forbidding glory, as well as several varieties of venomous snakes, and she shuddered at the thought of the early pioneers who had had to cut away that undergrowth in order to found the first big sheep and cattle stations. It must have taken a hardy breed. Men like John's grandfather, who'd founded the Sterling Run.

She glanced at the hard lines of his craggy broad face, and her eyes lingered helplessly on his wide chiseled mouth before she could drag them back to the window. That hard expert mouth had taught hers every single thing it knew about kissing . . .

She moved restlessly in the seat as the car wound over the gap in the range and they began descending again. In the distance were rolling grasslands that spread out to the horizon, to the great outback in the western part of the state, which was called the Channel Country. John had cousins out there, she knew.

Southwest of Brisbane were the Darling Downs, the richest agricultural land in Queensland. But northwest were some of the largest cattle stations in Australia, and that was where Providence sat, along a river that provided irrigation for its three sheep and cattle stations. One of those was the Sterling Run.

Priss wanted to ask why John was driving a Ford. It occurred to her that he'd had a silver Mercedes when she'd left Australia. He'd driven the Mercedes when he was going to town, and a Land-Rover on the station. But then, she also wondered about his clothing. John had always worn a suit to town, and it had usually been an expensive one. She laughed bitterly to herself. Probably he didn't feel he needed to waste his time dressing up for her. Her eyes closed. If she'd been Janie Weeks, no doubt he'd have been dressed to the back teeth. She wondered whatever had happened to seductive Janie, and why John hadn't married her. Priss knew her mother would have told her if he had.

"Turn on the radio, if you like," he said shortly.

"No, thanks," she replied. "I don't mind peace and quiet. After Monday, I'll probably never know what it is again."

He glanced at her through a cloud of cigarette smoke, his blue eyes searching.

"Why is it that you're here before summer?" he asked curiously. "The new term won't start until after vacation."

"One of the school staff had to have surgery. I'll be filling in until vacation time," she returned. "Ronald is going to work as a supply teacher, too, until we both have full-time positions next year."

He didn't reply, but he looked unapproachable. She wondered at the change in him. The John Sterling she used to know had been an easygoing, humorous man with twinkling eyes and a ready smile. What a difference there was now!

"Dad said something about Randy being at the station now; he and Latrice," she murmured, mentioning John's brother. "Are the twins with them?"

"Yes, Gerry and Bobby," he replied. "You'll be teaching them."

"How nice."

He looked sideways and laughed shortly.

"You haven't been introduced yet," he said enigmatically.

"What happened to Randy's own station in New South Wales?" she continued.

"That's his business," he said carelessly.

She flushed. It was mortifying to be told to mind her own affairs, and she resented his whole manner. "Excuse me," she replied coldly. "I'll keep my sticky nose to myself."

"Why did you come back?" he asked, and there was a note in his voice that chilled her.

"Why don't you do what you just told me to and mind your own business?" she challenged.

His head turned, and his eyes glittered at her. "You'll never fit in here," he said, letting his gaze punctuate the words. "You're too much the sophisticate now."

"In your opinion," she returned with faint humor. "Frankly, John, your opinion doesn't matter beans to me these days."

"That goes double for me," he told her.

So it was war, she thought. Good. This time she was armed, too. She ran a hand through her short hair. "Does it look like it'll be a dry year?" she asked, changing the subject.

"No. They're predicting a good bit of rain when the Wet comes. The past two years have been good to us."

"That's nice to know."

"Yes, there have been some lean times

. . . look out!" He braked suddenly for a kangaroo. The tawny beast bounded right into the path of the car and stared at its occupants, with a tiny baby in its pouch. John had stopped only inches from it, cursing a blue streak, and the kangaroo simply blinked and then hopped off to the other side of the highway.

"I'd forgotten about the "'roos," Priss laughed, grateful that she'd been wearing her seat belt. "They're bad pedestrians."

"That one bloody near met its maker," he returned on a rough sigh. "Are you all right?" he asked with obvious reluctance.

"Of course."

He started off again, and Priss stretched lazily, unaware of his eyes watching the movement with an odd expression in their azure depths.

He seemed content to sit there smoking his cigarette, and Priss kept her own silence. She wondered at her composure. Several years ago riding alone in a car with John would have been tantamount to backing the winner in the Melbourne Cup race. Now she was so numb that only a trickle of excitement wound through her slender body. Perhaps even that would go away in time.

Eventually they came to Providence, which looked very much the same, a small oasis of buildings among the rolling grasslands with the hazy ridges of the Great Dividing Range in the distance behind them and eternity facing them. John turned off the main bitumen road onto a graveled track that led past the Sterling Run on the way to Priss's parents' home. She tried not to look, but her eyes were drawn helplessly to the big sprawling house with its wide porches and colonial architecture. The driveway was lined with oleanders and royal poinciana and eucalyptus trees, which everyone called simply gum trees. Streams crisscrossed the land. They mostly dried up in the nine months preceding the Wet, which came near Christmas, but when the Wet thundered down on the plains, it was possible to be confined to the house for days until the rains stopped. Once she and her parents had had to stay with the Sterlings or be drowned out, and their small house had suffered enormous water damage.

"The house looks as if it has just been painted," she remarked, noticing its gleaming white surface.

"It has," he said curtly.

She loved its long porches, where she had sat one spring with John's mother and watched the men herd sheep down the long road on their way to the shearing sheds. That would be coming soon, she recalled, along with dipping and vetting and the muster of the cattle that supplemented John's vast sheep herds.

Beyond the house and its grove of eucalyptus trees were the fenced paddocks where the big Merino sheep grazed. They'd just been moved, she imagined, because the paddocks looked untouched. She noticed that the fences looked different.

"There's so little wire," she remarked, frowning.

"Electrified fencing," John said. "Just one of the improvements we're making. It's less expensive than barbed wire or wooden fences."

"What if the power goes out?" she asked.

"We have backup generators," he returned. He glanced at her. "And men with shotguns . . ." he added with just a glimpse of his old dry humor.

But she didn't smile. The days were gone when she could do that with John. She only nodded.

Soon they were at her parents' house, deserted because Adam and Renée apparently hadn't come home yet.

"They'll be back by dark, they said," he told her.

She nodded, staring at the lovely little bungalow, with its high gabled roof and narrow long front porch and green shutters at the windows. It was set inside a white picket fence, and Priss loved the very look of it, with the gum trees towering around it. Behind it was a stretch of paddock and then another grove of gum trees where a stream ran hidden, a magic little glade where she liked to watch koala bears feed on eucalyptus leaves and wait for lorikeets and other tropical birds to alight briefly on their flights.

"It looks just the same," she remarked softly.

He got out and removed her bag from the trunk. She followed him onto the porch, and as she looked up her green eyes suddenly flashed with the memory of the last time they'd been alone together at this house.

He searched her eyes slowly. "It was a long time ago," he said quietly.

"Yes," she agreed, her face clouding. "But I haven't forgotten. I'll never forget. Or forgive," she added coldly.

He stuck his hands into his pockets, staring down at her from his formidable height. "No," he said after a minute, and his voice was deep and slow. "I could hardly expect that, could I? It's just as well that it's all behind us. You and I were worlds apart even then."

Her knees felt rubbery, but she kept her poise. "Thank you for bringing me home," she said formally.

"I won't say it was a pleasure," he returned. "For my part, I wish you'd never come back."

He turned, and she glared after him with her heart going wild in her chest. She wanted to pick up something and throw it at him! But she stood there staring after him furiously and couldn't even think of a suitable parting shot. She stood on the porch and watched him turn the car and drive away in a cloud of dust. Then she turned and read the welcoming note on the door before she turned the knob and went inside.

It took only a minute to regain her familiarity with the comfortable furnishings and warm feeling of the house. She thought she even smelled freshly baked apple pie. Her bedroom was still the same, and her eyes lingered helplessly on the bed. If only she could forget!

She dressed in a pair of designer jeans and a yellow sweater Aunt Margaret had given her as part of her graduation present, a complete new wardrobe. Then, determined to exorcise the ghosts, she walked out behind the house over the grassy deserted paddock down to the wooden fence that separated her father's property from John's.

With a long sigh, she leaned against the old gray wood. She could still see herself as a teenager, in those long-ago days when she'd haunted this spot, hoping for a glimpse of John Sterling. How carefree she'd been. How full of love and hope and happy endings. Happy endings that had never come.

Chapter Two

$\mathcal{I}$t was an Australian spring day when Priss went speeding across the empty paddock toward the fence that separated her father's small holding from John Sterling's enormous cattle station. She was flushed with excitement, her long silvery blonde hair fanning all around her delicate features as she ran, her green eyes sparkling.

"John!" she called. "John, I got it!"

The tall blond man on the big black gelding wheeled his mount, frowning impatiently for an instant at the sight of Priscilla risking life and limb. Barefoot, for God's sake, in a white sundress that would have raised a young man's temperature.

"Watch where you're going, girl!" he called back in his broad Australian drawl.

She kept coming, laughing, making a perfectly balletic leap onto the faded white wooden fence that separated the properties. In her slender hand, she was waving a letter.

"Keep going, mates, I'll catch up," he told his men, trying not to notice the amused looks on their faces as he rode toward the girl.

Priss watched him coming with the same adoration she'd given him freely for two years. She knew he was aware of her infatuation—he couldn't help being aware of it—but he indulged her to a point.

He was so rugged, she thought dreamily. Big and broad-shouldered, with hands almost twice the size of her own, he filled out his moleskins and chambray shirt with delicious flair. He was almost ugly. His nose was formidable, his bushy eyebrows jutted over heavy-lidded sapphire eyes that were almost transparent. His cheekbones were high, his mouth wide and sexy-looking, his chin stubborn and dimpled. His hair wasn't truly blond, either. It was light brown, with flaring blond highlights, like his eyebrows and the thick hair over his chest and brawny forearms. But despite his lack of sophisticated good looks, he suited Priss. She only wished, for the hundredth time, that she suited him. He was still a bachelor at twenty-eight, but women liked him. He had an easygoing, humorous manner that appealed to most people, although he had a formidable temper when riled.

"Barefoot again," he said curtly, glaring at Priss's pretty little feet on the fence rail. "What am I going to do with you?"

"I could make several suggestions," she murmured with a mischievous smile.

He lit a cigarette, not commenting, and leaned his forearms over the pommel of the saddle. His sleeves were rolled up, and Priss's helpless eyes were drawn to the huge muscular hands holding the reins and the cigarette. The leather creaked protestingly as he sat forward to stare at her from under the wide brim of his Stetson. "Well, what's the news, little sheila?" he prompted.

"I got the scholarship," she told him proudly, eyes twinkling.

"Good on you!" he said.

"Mom's proud," she said. "And Dad's especially pleased because he teaches, too. I'm going to major in elementary education."

He studied her. Anyone would be less likely to become a teacher, he thought. He smiled softly. With her long hair curling like that, a silvery cloud around her delicate features, she was a vision. There wouldn't be any shortage of suitors. That disturbed him, and the smile faded. She was still a child. Just eighteen. His eyes went slowly over her slender body, to the taut thrust of her perfect breasts against the sundress's thin top, down over a small waist and slender hips and long elegant legs to her bare pretty feet.

Priss watched him, too, vaguely excited by the way he was looking at her. She couldn't remember a time before when he'd looked at her like that, as if she were a woman instead of an amusing but pesky kid.

She shifted on the fence, with the forgotten letter still clutched in one hand. "Will you miss me when I'm gone?" she asked, only half teasing.

"Oh, like the plague," he agreed, tongue in cheek. "Who'll drag me to the phone in the middle of calving to ask if I'm busy? Or go swimming in my pond just when I've stocked it with fish? Or ride me down in the woods when I'm taking a few minutes to myself?"

She dropped her eyes. "I guess I have been a pest," she agreed reluctantly. She brushed her hair back. "Sorry."

"Don't look so lost. I will miss you," he added, his voice soft and slow.

She sighed, looking up into his eyes. "I'll miss you, too," she confessed. Her eyes were eloquent, more revealing than she knew. "Hawaii's so far away."

"It was your choice," he reminded her.

She shrugged. "I got carried away by the scenery when I toured the campus with Aunt Margaret. Besides, having an aunt nearby will make things easier, and you know Mom and Dad don't want me living on campus. I kind of wish I'd decided on Brisbane, though."

"You're an American," he reminded her. "Perhaps you'll fit in better in Honolulu."

"But I've lived in Australia for two years," she said. "It's home now."

He lifted the cigarette to his mouth. "You're young, Priss. Younger than you realize. So much can change, in so little time."

She glared at him. "You think I'm just a kid, too. Well, mister, I'm growing fast, so look out. When I come back home for good, you're in trouble."

His bushy eyebrows lifted over amused eyes. "I am?"

"I'll have learned all about being a woman by then," she told him smugly. "I'll steal your heart right out of that rock you've got it embedded in."

"You're welcome to give it a go," he told her with a grin. "Fair dinkum."

She sighed. There he went again, humoring her. Couldn't he see her heart was breaking?

"Well, I'd better get back," she sighed. "I have to help Mom with lunch." She peeked up at him, hoping against hope that he might offer to let her come up behind him on his horse. It would be all of heaven to sit close against that big body and feel its heat and strength. She'd been close to him so rarely, and every occasion was a precious memory.

Now there wasn't a lot of time left to store up memories. Her heart began to race. Maybe this time . . .

"Mind your feet," he said, nodding toward them. "And look out for Joe Blakes."

She frowned, then remembered the rhyming slang he liked to tease her with. "Snakes!" she produced, "you Bananabender!"

He threw back his blond head and laughed, deeply and heartily. "Yes, I'm a Queenslander, that's the truth. Now on with you, little sheila, I've got work to do, even if you haven't."

"Yes, Your Worship," she mocked, and jumped down from the fence to give him a sweeping curtsy. Her eyes twinkled as he made a face. "That's called cutting tall poppies down to size!"

"I'm keeping score," he warned softly.

"How exciting," she replied tartly.

He laughed to himself and turned his mount. "Mind your feet!" he called again, amusement deepening his voice, and with a tip of his hat, he rode off as if he hadn't a care in the world. Priss watched him until he was out of sight among the gum trees, and sighed wistfully. Oh, well, there was still a week before she left for Hawaii. If only he'd kiss her. She flushed, biting her lower lip as the intensity of emotion washed over her. He never had touched her, except to hold her hand occasionally to help her up and down from perilous places. And once, only once, he'd lifted her and carried her like a child over a huge mud puddle when it was raining. She'd clung to him, as if drowning in his sensuous strength. But those episodes were few and far between, and mostly she survived on memory. She had a snapshot of him that she'd begged from his mother, on the excuse of painting him from it. The painting had gone lacking, but she had the photograph tucked in her wallet, and she wove exquisite daydreams around it.

With a world-weary look on her face, she got down from the fence and began to walk slowly back across the paddock. Maybe a snake would bite her, and she'd be at death's door, and John would rush to her bedside to weep bitter tears over her body. She shook herself. More likely, he'd pat the snake on the head and make a pet of it.

She wandered lazily back to the house and walked slowly up the steps to the cool front porch where she liked to sit and hope that John would ride by. In the distance were the softly rolling paddocks where John's Hereford cattle and big merino sheep grazed peacefully.

Her eyes grew sad as she realized that she would soon be far away from this dear, familiar scene. College. Several years of college in Hawaii—out of sight and sound and touch of

John Sterling. And he didn't even seem to mind. Not one bit.

Renée Johnson looked up as her daughter came into the house. She smiled a little as she bent her silver head again to her embroidery. She was in her late forties, but traces of beauty were still evident in her patrician face.

"Hello, darling; back already?" she teased.

"John was busy," Priss sighed. She plopped down into a chair with a rueful smile. "He's glad I'm leaving, you know."

"Oh, I don't think he is, really," Renée said carelessly. "Friendship can survive a few absences, dear."

Friendship. Priss almost wailed. She was dying of love for him!

"Dad should be back now, shouldn't he?" she asked.

"He had to stop in Providence to pick up his new suit on the way back from Brisbane," she reminded her daughter. "And Brisbane is a good drive from here."

"All for a student he hardly knows," Priss remarked. "Just because he needed a way to the airport. Dad's all heart, isn't he?"

"Yes, he is," her mother agreed warmly. "That's why I married him, you know."

Priss got up and paced the room. "I wonder if I'm doing the right thing. Hawaii's so far away . . ."

"The university there is one of the best," she

was reminded. "And your aunt will love having you close by. She's your father's favorite sister, you know."

"Yes." Priss stared out the window at the distant white cloud of moving sheep. John had cattle, too, but his primary interest was his big merino sheep. She loved watching the jackeroos move them from paddock to paddock. She loved the sheepdogs, so deft and quick. But most of all she loved John. John!

"Set the table, dear, would you?" Renée asked. "I'll be dishing up supper any minute."

Chapter Three

Adam Johnson glanced curiously at his daughter over the dinner table. It wasn't like Priscilla to pick at her food.

"Aren't you hungry, darling?" he asked.

She lifted her face with a plaintive smile. "I'm just homesick already," she confessed.

"Homesick? Don't be silly, Hawaii's not that far away," he chuckled. "You can come home on holidays and vacation."

She pushed her fork into her potatoes and stared at them. "I suppose so."

Adam turned his head toward Renée, who was shaking her head.

"It's just . . . well, do you suppose John really will miss me?" she asked her father, all eyes.

He laughed, misreading the situation. "Now, darling, I doubt that," he chuckled as he concentrated on his food. "You do wear him out, you know."

Priss got up from the table in tears and ran for her room. Her mother glared at her father.

"You animal," she accused. "How could you do that to her? Don't you realize she's horribly infatuated with John?"

His eyebrows arched. "With John? But, my God, he's ten years older than she is. And she's just a child!"

"She's eighteen," she reminded him. "Not a child at all."

"Well, John's too experienced for her by far," he said firmly. "Don't get me wrong—I think the world of him. But she needs boys her own age. And you know how relentlessly she chases the poor man, Renée. I wonder that he tolerates it. You can see he isn't interested in kids like Priss."

"Yes, I know. But she's so young, darling," Renée said softly. "Don't you remember how we felt at her age?"

His dark eyes softened. "Yes," he said reluctantly, and sighed. "With everybody around telling us how young we were. . . . poor Priss."

"She'll get over him," Renée promised. "Once she's with boys her own age, she'll get over him."

Priss, standing frozen in the hall, heard every word. It all came rushing at her like a tidal wave. Had she hounded John? Did *he* realize how desperately infatuated she was?

Her face flamed. She leaned back against the cool wall, almost shaking. Of course he did. Ten years, her father had said. John wouldn't want a child like herself. She closed her eyes. It was far worse than she'd realized. And the worst thing of all was that she hadn't realized how very noticeable her infatuation was. But it didn't feel like infatuation. She loved John!

She turned and went back into her room, closing the door quietly. She felt more alone than she ever had in her life. Poor John. Poor her. Her father had said John was too experienced to want a teenager, and he was surely right. If John had felt anything for her, he wouldn't have been able to hide it. She would have known. People always said you knew when love happened.

She tumbled onto her bed and slowly pulled out the crumpled photo of him that she kept in her wallet. She stared at it for a long time, at the rugged face, the bushy blond and brown eyebrows and hair, at the sensuous mouth and dimpled chin, at the pastel blue eyes. No, he wouldn't miss her, she thought miserably.

"Well, you don't know what you're losing, John Sterling," she told the photograph. "I'm going to be a force to behold in a few years, and you'll be sorry you didn't want me. I'll show you!" She put the photograph in her trash can in a temper and flounced over to the window, glaring out at the big gum tree casting its shade over the ground. She leaned her face on her hands and sighed. "I'll come back as finished as a princess," she told the gum tree. "I'll be wearing an elegant gown, with my hairdo impeccable, and I'll be poised and ever so serene. And every man will want to dance with me, and John will be wild to, and I'll just brush past him and ignore him completely."

She smiled as she pictured it. What a proper revenge it would be! But then she realized how impossible it was going to be, living through those years without him. And where would she get the money for an elegant gown and hairdo? And what if John got married in her absence?

She felt sick. With a scowl, she fished his photo out of the trash can and put it carefully back into her wallet. She had too much time to think, that was her trouble. So she went to the kitchen and began clearing the table for her mother, trying to ignore the curious looks her parents were giving her.

"Could we all go into Providence Saturday and have lunch together?" she asked with a forced smile. "I have to leave for Hawaii Monday, you know."

Her father gave a relieved sigh. "Yes, of course we can. That's a date."

"I'll enjoy it, too, dear." Her mother smiled. "Now, suppose I help you with the dishes and then we'll go sit on the porch."

"Fine," Priss said brightly. Perhaps the pretense of being happy would lighten her spirits, she thought. Perhaps it would dull her hurt. Why, oh, why did she have to pick a man like John Sterling to fall in love with, and at such a youthful age? He was going to be a ghost, hanging over every relationship she tried to have with other men. She knew that no one would be able to match or top him in her loving eyes.

She avoided him during the next few days. For once she didn't phone him to ask unnecessary questions at night. She didn't walk along the paddock fence hoping for a glance of him. She didn't find an excuse to ride her bicycle over the distance that separated her father's land from John's, or invite herself to lunch with his mother, Diane. She kept to herself, and her parents seemed delighted by the sudden maturity in their daughter.

They couldn't know that it was killing her not to see John, to think of being thousands of miles away from him. But she was deliberately trying to put him out of her life, so that the parting wouldn't be so rough.

The hours and days dragged, but at last Monday came, and she packed for the long drive to Brisbane, where she'd catch her flight to Hawaii. It was the most miserable morning of her entire life.

"Aren't you even going to tell John Sterling good-bye?" Renée asked, her face concerned and full of love.

Priss's back stiffened a little, but her face was smiling when she glanced at her mother. "I thought it might be better not to," she said.

"Why?"

Priss shrugged. Her eyes went to her folded blouses. She fit them carefully into her carry-on bag. "I don't think I could stand having him shout for joy," she said with a nervous laugh.

Renée went close and put her arms around her daughter. "Not John. John wouldn't do that to you. He's fond of you, Priss; you know that."

"Yes, but fond isn't enough," Priss ground out, fighting tears. She lifted a tortured face to her mother. "I love him," she whispered.

Renée hugged her. "Yes, I know. I'm so sorry, darling," she murmured, rocking Priss as she had years ago, when her daughter was little and hurt. "I'm so sorry."

Priss hugged her mother again and smiled wanly. "You're a terrific mother, did I ever tell you?" she asked. She wiped away the tears. "I'm okay now."

"You're a terrific daughter," Renée said with a smile. "I'll leave you to pack. Your father and I are going into Providence for a little while. He's got to get something or other done to the car."

"Okay. Be careful."

"We will." Renée kissed her daughter on the forehead. "It gets better, if that helps," she added gently. And then she was gone, and Priss stared helplessly at the suitcase, hating it for its very purpose.

She finished putting in the blouses and went into the kitchen to check the dryer for spare articles. She found a lacy slip and was just pulling it out when she heard a car pull up. Surely it wasn't her parents, she puzzled; they'd hardly been gone ten minutes.

She went to the back door, opened it, and looked out. Her heart shot up into her throat at the sight of John Sterling climbing out of his Land-Rover.

He was wearing khaki trousers with a short-sleeve tan bush shirt, and under the wide brim of his hat, he looked even more formidable than usual. Priss, with her hair loose around her shoulders, in her pretty blue shirtwaist dress and white pumps, felt suddenly vulnerable.

He looked up as he reached the steps and stopped there, just gazing at her.

"You've been avoiding me," he said without preamble.

She twisted the slip absently in her fingers and studied the soft pattern in the lace. "Yes."

She glanced up with a forced grin. "Aren't you relieved? I'll be gone by afternoon."

He hesitated for an instant before he came up the steps. "Got something cool to drink?" he asked, sweeping off his hat. "It's damned hot."

"I think there's some iced tea in the fridge," she said. She tossed the slip onto the dryer and filled a glass for him.

He took it from her, standing much too close. He was scowling, as if his mind was working on some problem. He took a sip of the tea, and her eyes were drawn to his brawny hair-roughened forearms. He was so sexy, and some lucky woman was going to grab him up before she was old enough to.

She felt more miserable than ever. She'd promised herself she wasn't going to cry, even if he did manage to get over to say good-bye. But now it was the eleventh hour, and he'd be rushing off any minute. He was probably here to see her father, anyway.

"Did you want to see Dad?" she asked, turning the knife in her own heart.

"I wanted to see you," he corrected curtly. "To say good-bye. Weren't you even going to bother?"

She shrugged, staring down at his dusty boots. "I . . . I don't like good-byes," she managed in a voice that was already starting to break. The thought of not seeing him for months was killing her, and this was making it worse. She didn't know how she was going to live in a world without him.

"What's this?" he asked softly. His big hands, cool from holding the tea glass, caught her arms and turned her, forcing her to look at him.

Her full lips wobbled no matter how she tried to control their trembling, and her big emerald eyes were misty with tears. Silvery blonde hair curled around her oval face, and her cheeks were flushed with emotion. The picture she made held his attention for a long minute. His eyes wandered down to the top buttons of the blue shirtwaist dress, and he studied her body as if he'd only just realized she had one.

His hands smoothed up and down her arms, slowly, making wild tremors of pleasure shoot through her.

"Homesick already?" he asked quietly.

She drew in a sharp breath and tried to smile at him, but he blurred in her vision.

He was a blur of brown hair with blond streaks through it, sky blue eyes staring curiously at her from that weathered face that she loved so dearly. It was a long way to look up, even though she was wearing high heels. He towered over her like a sunburned giant.

"You're so big," she whispered.

"To a runt like you, I probably seem that

way," he agreed pleasantly, but his eyes weren't laughing. They were dark and quiet and oddly watchful.

She fidgeted under the arousing touch of his hands. "I should finish packing," she mumbled.

His thumbs pressed hard into her arms. He moved his callused hands up to enclose her face, and the look in his eyes made her knees weak.

"Don't look so tragic, darling," he murmured, bending his head. "I'll wait for you."

That hurt most of all. He was teasing her, playing with her, because he knew how she felt and was indulging her. Her eyes closed. "John . . ." she tried to protest.

He brushed his lips across her forehead, and she wanted to wail. He was trying not to hurt her. . . .

"Do you want my mouth, little sheila?" he whispered suddenly, unexpectedly, and her heart shot up like a balloon.

Her eyes opened, full of dreams and hurt pride and aching hunger, and his nostrils flared.

"Yes, you do, don't you?" he asked under his breath, and his face was solemn, intent, making her feel years older. He bent his head, letting her feel his warm breath on her parted lips.

Her body tautened, demanding to feel his

against it; her mouth lifted. All her dreams were coming true at once, and the look in his eyes made her heart run wild. Her body pressed against his tentatively, shyly. She loved his warm strength, the powerful muscles tensing where her breasts were flattened slightly against him. He smelled of the outdoors, and cologne and tobacco, and her senses reeled.

"I've only been kissed once," she whispered nervously, her eyes wide. "Playing . . . playing spin the bottle. And his mouth was wet and I didn't like it."

His fingers traced soft patterns on her flushed cheek, and they seemed to be the only two people in the world. "Stop dithering, little one," he said quietly. "I don't mind kissing you good-bye, if you want it."

"If," she whispered shakily. Tears were stinging her eyes. "Don't you know that I'd walk across blazing coals to get to you . . . ?"

His eyes flashed. "You don't even know what it's all about," he said sharply. "One kiss, from a clumsy boy . . ."

"But you aren't a boy," she reminded him, her voice trembling.

"No," he said, "I'm not." He bent slowly, holding her eyes. "Such a taut little body," he breathed, his hard lips parting on a faint smile as they brushed deliciously over hers. "Why don't you let it relax against mine?"

She tried, but she was trembling with excitement and new discoveries. "I can't," she moaned against the soft persistent brushing of his mouth.

His fingers splayed over her throat, tilting her head against his shoulder. "I'm hungry, too," he whispered roughly. There was a glitter in his eyes as they searched hers. "Don't let me frighten you. Trust me."

"I want to kiss you so much," she managed in a broken tone, so desperate for him that she was beyond pride.

"Yes," he said, parting his lips. "Yes, I can feel how much. Priss, you go to my head . . ." His voice trailed off into a deep slow moan as he kissed her for the first time, tenderly, coaxingly, letting her feel the very texture of his lips before he showed her that he needed more than this.

His breath seemed shaky as his mouth bit at hers. She kept her eyes tightly closed, hoping that if it was a dream, she could die before she woke. The silence around them was deafening, and she felt afire with awakening emotions.

Her hands suddenly clawed into the thick muscles of his upper arms, and she stiffened even more as his mouth began to invade hers. She hoped he wasn't going to waste her last few minutes with him by being gentle.

His head lifted then and his mouth waited,

poised over hers. His breath sighed out against her moist lips. "I can make you hungrier than this," he said huskily. "I can burn you up."

His eyes frightened her a little, but she was too consumed by longing to care. She pressed closer against his tight hard body and stood on tiptoe.

"Oh, John, kiss me hard!" she pleaded, clinging. "Kiss me hard and slow and pretend you want me!"

"Pretend!" he bit off. His mouth swooped down. He could feel the hunger building in her young body, feel the first faint stirring of response in the tender lips accepting his. Ravenously he opened his mouth and bit at hers, not wanting to frighten her, but needing more than the trembling uncertainty of her closed mouth. After a minute, she seemed to like the tender probing of his tongue. Involuntarily her lips relaxed and began to part shyly.

"Yes," he prodded roughly. "Yes, that's what I want. Open your mouth slowly; let me taste it with my tongue . . ."

It was wildly erotic. Priss had seen men and women kiss that way in movies, with their mouths open, their bodies crushed together, but she'd never known how wildly arousing it was. She moaned against John's demanding mouth, because the sensations he was making her feel were new and overwhelming.

"Frightened?" he whispered.

Her eyes drifted open, wide and drowsy and dazed. "No," she moaned. "Oh, no, not of you; not ever of you," she whispered shakily. "No matter what you do to me!"

"You don't know what I could do to you," he warned gruffly. He studied her face for a long moment. His hands smoothed down her back, bringing her closer to his shuddering chest. One of them edged between their bodies and traced a line between her waist and the soft underside of one breast. She trembled again, her fingers digging into him.

"Steady on," he breathed gently, watching her face as his fingers began to trace her breast, watching her eyes widen with pleasure.

She made a wild sweet sound and buried her face against his chest, clinging to him.

"I need this," he said, sounding shaken. "God help me, I have to!"

She felt his mouth searching for hers, and she turned her head a fraction of an inch to meet it.

"Keep your eyes open," he breathed as he took it, ardently, roughly, and his eyes stared into hers. His hand moved at the same time, and he saw her pupils dilate until her eyes were black as he cupped her soft breast in his big hand and felt the nipple go hard in his palm.

She moaned, feeling her body move helplessly against his, feeling her body provoke him, beg for his touch.

He lifted his mouth. "It's passion," he whispered. "Don't be ashamed of it. I need you as much as you need me. I won't compromise you—not in any way."

As he spoke, he bent, lifting her clear off the floor, his eyes glazed with emotion. "Where are your parents?" he asked softly as he carried her into her bedroom.

"In . . . in town, to have . . . to have the car . . . fixed," she told him. Her voice was so shaky, it was hard to talk. "John," she moaned.

"Shhh," he whispered. His lips brushed her eyelids closed. "It's going to be exquisitely tender I just want a taste of you."

"I've never . . ." she began.

"I know."

He laid her down beside the open suitcase on the bed and slid alongside her. His mouth touched her face softly, lovingly, brushing every flushed inch of it, teasing her mouth. She felt his knuckles on her soft flesh as they slid beneath the bodice of her dress, and her eyes opened, because what he was teaching her was so beautiful, she wanted to remember him like this all her life. Even if it was only pity he felt for her, she'd live on these few minutes until she died.

"I'm only going to touch you," he said gently. "Here," he whispered, tracing the slope of her breast where it was covered by the lacy wisp of her bra. "And here." They moved under the lace, to the hard pulsing tip that screamed her helpless reaction to him.

"Oh," she moaned, shocked, arching to his hand.

"New sensations?" he responded, savoring the feel of her, bursting with the triumphant knowledge that no other man had touched her. "I feel new sensations, too, Priss. You're a virgin, and all your first times are happening with me. I feel humble knowing that."

She stared into his eyes. "I wanted you . . . so much," she confessed brokenly.

His eyes smiled. "Did you? And now that you have me?"

Her lips parted. "I don't know what to do," she said simply.

"Do you want me to teach you?" His voice was all dark velvet, seducing her, and he smiled as his big hands found the buttons of her dress and lazily eased them open down the front.

"Yes," she entreated. "But . . ." Her courage failed as the last button came undone, and the full force of what she was letting him do washed over her in waves.

He shook his head, pressing a gentle finger against her protesting lips. "No," he said. "I don't want this to happen with some college boy, out of curiosity. Let me be the first."

Her body trembled. But she loved him almost beyond bearing, and she wanted his eyes on her. Only his. No other man's, ever.

His hands moved again, unfastening the bra. There was a second when she almost jerked away from him, but he controlled the instinctive withdrawal, pulling her face into his throat, making her close her eyes while he eased the garments down to her waist. She felt the cool air on her skin and his warm rough hands against her bare back, and her heart went crazy in her body.

"Now," he breathed, with his open mouth against her forehead. "Now let me look at you. Lie down, Priscilla, and let me see what you've shown no other man."

With breathless tenderness, he eased her back onto the coverlet and slowly his eyes feasted on her soft pink breasts with their hardened, uptilted tips. She flushed.

But after the first few agonizing seconds of embarrassment, she began to relax, to take pleasure from the appreciation she read in his intent gaze. Her body seemed to like it even more. It began to move in jerky sensuous motions on the mattress and lifted toward him without her consent.

"Do you want my hands?" he asked, lifting his eyes to hers.

She tingled all over, her breath catching in her throat at the deep, fervent note in his voice. His sophistication made her innocence more obvious than ever.

He sat up and one big hand smoothed across her flat stomach, across the bulge of the clothing at her waist. Lightly, slowly, holding her eyes, he touched the hard peaks of her breasts and watched her shudder.

"Your breasts are like honey," he said. "You're like honey. So sweet, you make me drunk." He bent, with his eyes on her bareness. "I want to take you in my mouth," he breathed. "Are you going to let me?"

She groaned helplessly, and her body arched again, inviting him.

"Priss," he whispered, sliding his hands slowly under her back. "Priss, come here."

He lifted her to his parted lips. She stiffened and cried out with the shock of pleasure as his mouth took her, and the excited little cry aroused him instantly. He took the hardness into his mouth and eased closer, feeling her reactions, glorying in her headlong response. Her hands tangled in his hair, frantic. Those wild little cries were pushing him right over the edge, making him shudder with a kind of desire he'd never experienced.

"Oh, God," he whispered with reverence, because she was so deliciously innocent, so trusting. She was giving him free license to do what he liked to her smooth young body, and he was going crazy with the freedom.

His mouth moved down her body, to her waist, her hips, the flatness of her stomach, as he eased the dress further down to bare her body to his greedy lips. She tasted of delicate soap and powder, and he wanted to taste all of her. . . .

"Do you want me now?" he whispered roughly. His mouth ran back up her body, over her creamy breasts to her face, and he cupped her breast as his lips made nonsense of any protest she might have made. "Do you want to lie with me and touch me the way I'm touching you with nothing between us except air?"

"I . . . ache," she said through parched lips, clinging, trembling.

"So do I," he said unsteadily. "You've taken my mind from me. Lie still, darling. Let me touch you, let me have you."

His face moved, touching, brushing. His mouth loved her, cherished her. She was shuddering under its tenderness, and he knew she'd make no further protest if he undressed her completely and took her. But even as he was drowning in the anguished pleasure of the knowledge, he began to think about consequences. She was a virgin. The first time for her was probably not going to be as good as it would be for him. He was more aroused than he'd ever been in his life—too aroused to take his time, to give her patience. And worst of all, she'd be unprotected. He could make her pregnant. It was that thought that brought him suddenly to his senses. She was hardly more than a child herself.

He dragged his mouth from her soft belly and managed to pull his tormented body into a sitting position, breathing roughly, running his hands through his damp hair. She was breathing roughly herself, and her body was trembling wildly.

With a harsh mutter, he brought her up into his arms and rocked her damp body against his. "Hold me hard, darling," he whispered into her ear, feeling the heat of her breasts through the cotton of his shirt. Her back under his hands was like silk. "Hold me. It will stop. Hold me hard."

She clung to him, vaguely embarrassed at the intensity of her response, wildly frustrated, wanting something he hadn't given her but not realizing exactly what.

"Oh, gosh," she whispered, awed.

"Now you know," he said gently.

Her nails bit into his shoulders, and she nuzzled her head into his neck, shuddering a little as her heartbeat calmed and her breath steadied. "You . . . weren't going to stop . . . at first. Why . . . did you?" It was a statement, not a question.

His big hand smoothed her hair slowly. "I could have made you pregnant."

Thrills of pleasure wafted through her. She might have liked that, being pregnant with his child. It wasn't at all frightening. But it would be a poor way of getting him, a mean trick. She sighed.

"I'd have let you," she answered.

He laughed softly. "Yes, I know. Delicious, delightful little virgin." He bit her shoulder, quite hard, and she shuddered with unexpected pleasure and laughed.

He half threw her back on the pillows and sat looking down at her seminudity with possessive, glittering blue eyes. "I've never wanted anyone so much," he said huskily. "I was on fire for you. I still am."

It was plain speaking, and a little embarrassing—like her wanton behavior. He seemed to sense those uncertainties, because he smiled tenderly when she sat up and began to tug her dress back in place.

"Don't be embarrassed," he said gently. "Only the two of us will ever know what happened here today." He touched her mouth with a long finger. "And I won't tell if you won't."

That was the John she loved so much, teasing, mischievous. She couldn't help smiling at him. He smiled back and bent, kissing her softly, amorously, as his hands drew the bodice down again. "I'll never see anything else so beautiful as long as I live," he ground out, staring at her pink skin where his mouth had pressed and pulled and tasted it, with something like reverence on his hard face.

She flushed wildly and blushed even there,

and he bent and kissed the shyness from her eyes, her mouth.

His fingers moved the damp hair away from her face, and he looked at her as if she were a sunrise he was committing to memory. "You belong to me now," he said quietly. "Keep your body for me, and no other man. I'll wait for you."

"It belonged to you long before now," she said in a choked tone, her eyes searching his. "John, I . . . !"

He put his fingers over her lips. "Don't say it." His mouth replaced his fingers, and he kissed her with an expertise that left her moaning, in tears, when he lifted his head. "You're very young," he said, as if it bothered him. "There's plenty of time."

"Plenty?" she queried. "When I'm leaving today?"

"Darling," he breathed, staring down at her, "if you weren't leaving today, you might damned well find yourself in my bed by nightfall."

He got to his feet, stretching lazily and indulgently watched her efforts to rearrange her dress. There was possession in his eyes, and quiet pride, but she wasn't looking.

"See what happens when you avoid me?" he asked as she got to her feet, smoothing back her disheveled hair. "Frustration can push a man to the very limits."

She smiled shakily. "Was that what it was?"

He caught her waist and pulled her to him. "What do you think it was?" he asked.

She stared at his shirt, curious about how he looked without it. She'd only seen him that way from a distance, when he was working on fences with the men or digging a new bore.

"It's too late now," he said deeply, his voice amused. "If you wanted to go on safari, you should have indulged yourself while we were lying together on the bed."

She flushed, and he laughed.

"The months will pass," he said lightly, giving her a last careless kiss. "Write to me."

"Could I?" she asked, breathless.

"Of course."

"Will you write back?"

He shifted from one foot to the other. "I'm not much good at letters, honey," he confessed. "I'll get Mother to write for me."

His words hurt her. They wouldn't be love letters—he was saying as much. Perhaps he'd meant what they had just shared as a going-away present, a fond farewell. Something to make up for the times when he'd ignored her, crumbs from his table.

She felt sick all over, but she was too proud to let it show. How could she have forgotten what her father had said, about John being glad to let her go, about his being too old to be interested in her?

"I'll see you at the Easter holidays," he said. "You'll be home then?"

"Of course," she said woodenly. "'Bye, John."

He traced her cheek lightly with his finger, and his eyes met hers in a long hot exchange, but he didn't touch her again. "'Bye, Priss. Keep well."

"You, too."

And he was gone, leaving her with the memory of a few wild minutes in his arms. It might have been kinder, she thought, if he'd spared her that. Coming from heaven back to earth was painful. She went to the window and watched him drive away. He waved from the end of the driveway, and she knew that he was aware of her watchful eyes. He knew how she felt. It had all been a pacifier, a consolation prize. Give the girl a few kisses to thrill her.

She went back to her suitcase and stared at it, denying her eyes the tears they wanted to shed. Well, she didn't need John's crumbs, thank you, she told herself. She'd go away and forget him. She'd forget him completely.

Sure, she would. She sat down on the bed and wailed. The coverlet still smelled of the spicy cologne he wore. Her lips touched it with aching passion, and it was a long time before she could force herself to get up and finish packing.

Hours later she said good-bye to her parents in Brisbane and climbed aboard a plane bound for the Hawaiian Islands. Despite the fact that she had promised herself she wouldn't, her helpless eyes scanned the airport terminal for a glimpse of John. But he wasn't there. Why should he be? He'd said his good-byes. She sat back in her seat and closed her eyes. It was going to be a long day.

Chapter Four

$\mathscr{P}$riss settled in at the University of Hawaii in Honolulu, on the island of Oahu, and found the diversity of cultures and races as fascinating as she'd found Australia. She lived off campus, with Aunt Margaret, and found her young-minded aunt a lively and delightful companion. When Priss wasn't attending classes, her aunt toured her around the island. Priss found breathtaking beauty in the beaches and mountains and volcanos and flowers, and day by day the hurt of leaving behind her family and the man she loved began to ease.

One of her biggest consolations was the new friend she'd found in Ronald George, a tall dark-haired Englishman with blue eyes who was studying for a degree in education, too.

Her introduction to him had come the first day of classes, when he'd sidled up to her in the auditorium and leaned down to whisper in her ear.

"I say," he asked conspiratorially, "would you be interested in having a blazing affair with me during algebra? It is a bit crowded in here right now, but I do see a place just behind the curtains in the auditorium . . ."

She'd looked up at him dumbfounded. "What?"

"Just a short affair," he continued. "Until second period class? All right, then, you've talked me into marriage. But you'll have to wait until I have an hour to spare. Say, around lunchtime?" He grinned. "I'm Ronald George, by the way. You'd have seen the name on our marriage certificate, but I thought you might like to know beforehand."

"You're incredible!" she burst out. She stared up at him while she decided between running for help or laughing aloud.

"Yes, and just think, you haven't even seen me in action yet!" He leered at her playfully. "How about it? Or we could become engaged now. The thing is, old girl, I don't have a ring on me. . . ."

She decided in favor of laughter. "Oh, stop, I'll hurt myself," she gasped after laughing until her stomach ached.

He brushed back a lock of his wavy dark hair. "I knew we'd hit it off. You're just my type. A girl."

She held out her hand. "I'm Priscilla Johnson, from Queensland, Australia."

"What an odd accent you have, if you don't mind my saying so," he commented. "Sort of southern Australian?"

"I'm from Alabama originally," she confessed. "My father teaches in Providence. That's a small town northwest of Brisbane, near several large stations."

"Ah, yes. Australia." He studied her with a warm smile. "I'd like to teach there myself, when I take my degree. Especially if that's where *you're* going to teach."

"It is." She smiled back. "Been here long?"

"Two whole nights," he said. "I miss the rain and the fog and the cold back home," he sighed.

"I left spring in Australia."

"I say, we'll probably both die in this island paradise," he predicted.

"I know a girl who's studying to be a doctor," she told him. "She'll save us once she gets through premed. You can't possibly catch pneumonia until then."

"Oh. Well, in that case, I shall put on a mustard plaster tonight. And perhaps a couple of hot dogs to keep it company."

The bell rang just as she was warming to him, but in the weeks and months that followed, they became fast friends. Both of them knew it wasn't going to be any mad romance, but they found they genuinely liked each other. And Priss needed a friend desperately. The longer she was away from John Sterling, the more she missed him. It became an actual pain to lie down at night and think about him.

By the time six months had passed and Easter rolled around, she'd had all too much time to think about how she'd hounded John for the last two years. It hadn't helped that Renée had written that John was riding around with Janie Weeks, a notorious divorcée in the district. It was probably nothing, Renée had written, but people were talking about it. Still, Priss was certain John was carrying on an affair and it hurt in an intolerable way.

She cried for hours after that, and her usually bright face was full of bitter hurt as she went to her sociology class just before school let out for Easter vacation.

"What's wrong, Priss?" Ronald asked her, his fond eyes concerned. "I say, you aren't breaking your heart over me, I hope?" He grinned. "Dying of unbridled passion . . . ?"

"Well, maybe," she teased. Then her face became serious. "I don't want to go home at Easter," she lied.

"Good!" he chuckled. "Stay here and I'll take you to a luau at my roommate's parents' home."

"That sounds like fun," she said. "Really?"

"Really. I've talked about you so much, Danny's dying to meet you."

Her eyes searched his. "Well . . ."

"Come on," he chided. "I'm not trying to talk you into anything. Just friends, as we agreed."

She relaxed. "Okay. I'll stay."

"Great!" he exclaimed. "I'll tell Danny you're coming. This is going to be a gala affair, old girl; they're even roasting a suckling pig I hear." He leaned down. "Not to worry, the pig had absolutely nothing left to live for—he'd only just been jilted by his girlfriend."

She burst out laughing. "Oh, you're good for me!"

"What did I tell you in the beginning?" he asked with a smug smile.

She relaxed a little then, because she had a concrete reason to stay in Hawaii. She didn't want to have to tell her parents the truth: that she was dying because John didn't care enough to write to her. That she couldn't bear to see him with another woman.

That night she called Renée and Adam from Margaret's house.

"Not coming home?" Renée gasped. "But, darling, we've made plans . . ."

"I'm sorry," she said, pretending cheerfulness, "but you remember I told you about Ronald George? Well, he's invited me to this big luau at his friend's home a couple of days from now, and he's such a nice guy . . . well, I said yes before I thought." She crossed her fingers against the lie.

"He's the British boy," Renée recalled. She sighed. "Priss, we've invited some people over tomorrow night, kind of a homecoming party for you. John was coming."

She closed her eyes on a wave of loneliness and love. "With his new lady, no doubt?" she grated.

There was a pause. "You don't understand," Renée began. "I need to explain—"

"Yes, I understand very well," Priscilla interrupted, sounding mature and sophisticated. "I had a wild crush on John, but being over here has cured me. I want someone younger, like Ronald, who can enjoy the things I do. I'm having such a good time, Mom. You don't really mind if I skip this one holiday, do you?"

"No, of course not," Renée said, "if it's what you really want."

"It is," Priscilla said firmly. "Is Dad there?"

"He's working late tonight, but I'll have him call you when he comes in if you like."

"No, don't. I'll call back in a day or so. Mom . . . ?" She wanted to ask about John—if he was healthy and if he might marry that new woman—but she didn't dare, not after the fabrications she'd just put forth. "I love you," she said instead.

"I love you, too, darling," Renée said. "Priss, about John . . ."

"That part of my life is over, and I'm sure he's glad," Priscilla said quietly. "It must be lovely for him, not being chased by me."

"He looks rather lonely, if you want to know," came the soft reply. "He asks about you all the time. He said you were supposed to write to him."

She felt hot and cold all at once. "He . . . didn't really want me to, you know. It was just that he felt sorry for me."

"I don't believe that."

"Mom, you and Dad have to meet Ronald," she said enthusiastically. "He comes from a very upper-crust British family. He's wildly intelligent and full of fun, and he's going to come back to Providence with me when we graduate to teach! Isn't that great? He's super. You and Dad will like him a lot."

Renée sighed heavily. "Yes, dear, I'm sure we will. You must bring him home with you sometime."

After that the conversation became general, and John wasn't mentioned again. But when Renée said good-bye and hung up, memories of him ran around and around in Priscilla's head until she wanted to scream. He'd made all those comments about waiting for her and putting his mark on her, but he hadn't meant them. Her mother was a hopeless romantic, and she loved John. It was no wonder she was still playing matchmaker. But Priss was through mooning over John Sterling. She was going to survive, one way or another, and close him out of her life and her heart. She was going to get over him.

The luau was wonderful, very Polynesian and exciting. Ronald's roommate, Danny, was Hawaiian, an intelligent young man with liquid brown eyes and a quick wit. Priss liked him immediately. And Danny's parents were as open and friendly as he was. Besides, several of the kids from college were there. Priss enjoyed herself. Yet part of her was still mourning John, as she had been since leaving Australia.

"Priss, you've been brooding for days," Ronald remarked as they strolled along the beach together. He glanced down at her in the late evening breeze, studying her drawn face. "It's a man, isn't it?"

She glanced at him and sighed. "Yes." She'd never told him about John. She couldn't talk to anyone about John, not even Aunt Margaret.

"Bad experience?"

"Nothing like that," she laughed softly. "I was madly infatuated and chased him, that's all. I'm still a little embarrassed about it."

"How did he feel?"

"Sorry for me."

"Oh." He reached out and caught her hand.

"I had the same thing happen, actually," he confided. "She doesn't know I'm alive."

"Have you considered putting a notice in the paper?" she asked, tongue in cheek.

He burst out laughing. "I don't think it would work. She doesn't read the paper." He wrinkled his eyebrows. "Confidentially, old girl, I'm not sure she can read. But, my, what a figure!"

"Poor old thing."

"I'll survive," he replied. He sighed, watching the whitecaps pound against the white sand. "People always love the wrong people."

"Yes, I know." She squeezed his hand. "But it's nice to have friends to console you."

He smiled. "Still sure you don't want to have a blazing affair with me?"

"Sorry. I'm just not one for blazing affairs. But I need all the friends I can get."

"Actually," he reflected, winking down at her, "I was going to say the same thing. It's nice having a female to talk to about other females. I wouldn't dare rock the boat!"

"You're a nice bloke," she said. "Does that sound Australian?" she added, all eyes. "I'm practicing."

"I say, jolly good!" he grinned. He frowned. "Does that sound British? I have to keep in practice, too, you know."

She laughed and tossed her hair in the breeze. The whole world smelled of salt sea air and tropical flowers, and she held on to his hand as they walked. It was lovely having him for a friend. If only she could forget about John and put him completely out of her mind. The thought of Janie Weeks wrapping her thin arms around the big Australian made Priss ill. What in the world did John see in that horrible man-eater? Priss's face fell. Probably someone as experienced as himself. He'd made a lot of remarks about Priss's age.

She stared at the gorgeous sunset with misty eyes. "Paradise," she said softly. "As much as I love it, sometimes I'd trade it all for a Queensland drought. Except for the rainy season in summer, we go dry most of the year."

"You mentioned it had been a dry summer back home," Ronald recalled.

"Yes. A lot of the station owners had setbacks. My parents told me John Sterling lost a lot of sheep and cattle. But I don't suppose it would bother him, with the numbers of animals he has."

"He'd be the man, I presume?" Ronald asked softly.

"Yes." She tossed back her hair. "The Sterling Run is enormous. But it was never the property that interested me. It was the man."

"Ever thought of telling him how you feel?"

She laughed shortly. "He knows how I feel. He's always known. He just doesn't care. He said he wasn't much good at writing letters, that he'd have his mother do it for him." She sighed bitterly. "Besides, he's been seen around the district with the local wild woman."

"So that's how it is."

"That's how it is." She tried to blot out the memory of that last day at home, but, as always, it haunted her.

"Poor kid," he comforted, and tightened his fingers.

"I'll get over him," she said. "All I need is a little time."

But as she lay in bed that night back at Aunt Margaret's house, she wondered if she was ever going to forget him. None of the boys at college, even Ronald, did a thing for her in any physical or emotional way. She was a one-man woman, and John was the one man. All the bravado in the world wasn't going to change that.

She tossed and turned, hearing over and over again her mother's voice telling her how lonely John seemed. Well, if he was lonely, why wouldn't he write?

Somewhere in the distance a phone rang, and minutes later Aunt Margaret's soft voice sounded outside the bedroom door. She opened it a crack and peeked in, all soft curling salt and pepper hair and brown eyes. She was like a feminine version of Adam Johnson, the only one of his two sisters who favored him.

"It's for you, darling," she said with a twinkle in her eyes. "Feel like talking to a man with a sexy voice?"

"I might as well," Priss said with a reluctant grin, "I'm not sleeping very well. Is it Ronald?"

"No," Margaret said. "Go ahead. Pick it up. I'll see you in the morning. Good night."

Puzzled, Priss lifted the receiver. "Hello?"

"You can't pick up a bloody pen and write me two lines?" John Sterling demanded.

Her heart went wild. "John!" she burst out, all her good resolutions forgotten, her pride in ashes immediately at just the sound of his voice. She twisted the cord in her nervous fingers. "Oh, John, I miss you so much!"

There was a brief pause while she tried to regain her lost composure.

Damn, I've done it again, she thought furiously. She composed herself. "I miss everyone at home," she amended. "But it's great here, John, lots of sunshine and things to do, and places to see—"

"Stop rambling. Are you still dressed?"

She forced humor into her voice. "Why? Are you getting kinky? Want me to describe my night attire?"

"Stop that. I'm having hell trying to straighten things out at the station and worrying myself sick over you all at once. I bought a plane ticket I couldn't afford, and it wasn't just to hear you make cute remarks. How soon can you get here?"

Her mind went blank. "Get where? To Australia, you mean?"

"To the airport in Honolulu, dammit," he ground out.

Her jaw dropped. "You're here?"

"Yes, I'm here. Tired and hungry and half out of sorts—darling, get a move on, will you? And ask Margaret if I can stay the night. I have to talk to you."

It was heaven. Dreams drifting down. The end of the rainbow. She cried huge hot tears and laughed through them. "I can be there in twenty minutes," she said. "If I have to run all the way . . . !"

He caught his breath. "Hurry, darling," he said. "I'll wait."

She kissed the mouthpiece tenderly and hung it up, suspended for a moment in a world that had nothing to do with reality. Then she sprang out of bed and burst into Margaret's room.

"It's John; he's here; can he stay the night? We can put him on the sofa, and I have to get to the airport . . . !" It all tumbled out in a mad rush.

Margaret, who'd never married but remembered her own special season of love, smiled tolerantly. "Yes, he can stay the night. Get a cab to the airport—there's money in my pocketbook in the hall. Blankets in the closet. Now I'm going to sleep. Soundly," she added. "But don't take advantage of my complicity, dear."

Priss flushed. "No, I'd never do that," she promised. "Oh, Aunt Margaret, I love you," she said, impulsively hugging the older woman.

"I love you, too, dear. Now scoot!"

Priss was dressed in record time, in a pullover T-shirt and jeans and sneakers. She barely took time to run a brush through her hair, called a cab, and sat on the front steps of the small house waiting impatiently for it to come. Palm trees were silhouetted against the streetlights; the breeze rustled. And Priss was in agony. John was just miles away. John, here in Hawaii! The long months they'd been apart felt like years.

The cab came, at last, and she sat rigidly in the back until they got to the airport. She took just time enough to pay the driver before she went scurrying into the terminal.

Her wide soft eyes searched the crowd frantically. It wasn't until she felt the touch on her shoulder that she realized John wouldn't be wearing work clothes.

She turned, and there he was. All majesty and sophistication in a gray vested suit, his blond-streaked brown hair gleaming in the light, his face rigid, his eyes burning with blue sparks.

"Priss," he said in a tone that melted her knees.

"Oh, I thought I was dreaming," she remarked. Her lower lip trembled. "John, I'm sorry, but it hasn't changed, I haven't changed, I . . ."

He held out his arms, and she went into them like a homing pigeon, burying her face against his vest. His arms hurt, he was holding her so tightly, and she didn't even care.

She nestled her cheek on the soft fabric with a loud sigh. Her hands smoothed over the taut muscles of his back, under his suit coat. His heartbeat at her ear sounded heavy, rushed. She smiled, savoring it.

"No questions?" he asked quietly. "Don't you want to know why I'm here?"

"Eventually," she affirmed with a smile. Her chest rose and fell against him.

He laughed, although it sounded a little strained. "Let's go, honey."

"Didn't you bring a suitcase?" she asked as he put her gently away from him.

"I didn't have time. Not after Renée told me about that damned college kid," he said, and his eyes burned down into hers.

Her eyes widened as she read the stark jealousy in his expression. "You mean Ronald?" she asked, dazed.

He stared pointedly at her slender body. "Have you slept with him yet?"

Her lips parted. "No!" she gasped. "Of course not!"

"Why, of course not?" he demanded.

Her eyes softened as they searched his rugged face. "Because I belong to you, of course," she said with quiet pride. "I don't want another man's hands on me, ever."

He seemed to freeze in place. The breath he took was ragged. He touched her face with slow unsteady fingers. "I want you," he said huskily.

She managed a smile of her own. "I want you, too."

"Is Margaret asleep?" he asked.

She nodded.

He looked around. "Let's get out of here. I want to be alone with you."

She slid her hand into his big callused one, and let him lead her out of the terminal.

Minutes later they were in Margaret's plush living room, staring at each other in a momentary daze.

"I wanted to wait," he said. "I wanted to give you time, to let you see something of the world."

"Why?"

He shrugged his broad shoulders and glowered at her. "You're only eighteen."

She grinned. "Just the right age," she replied. "You can teach me."

"God, the thought of it makes me go weak in the knees," he laughed, staring at her. "Come here, you little torment, and let me love you."

She ran to him, glorying in his strength as he lifted her completely off the floor and laid her down on Margaret's green upholstered sofa. She sank into it, stretching with delicious anticipation while he shed his jacket and vest and slowly, sinuously, unbuttoned his shirt.

She'd seen him without it before, but that was a lifetime ago. The expanse of rippling bronze muscles excited her.

"Hurry up," she whispered impishly.

He grinned, his teeth white in his dark face. "Patience, darling."

She arched delicately, letting him see the thrust of her breasts through the thin material. He reached down and jerked the T-shirt up, baring her body to him. She hadn't bothered with a bra.

Her lips parted. "Yes, I like that," she whispered as he stared blatantly at her. "I like you looking at me."

"I'm going to do more than look."

"Be still, my throbbing heart," she teased, although her heartbeat *was* going wild.

He bent his head, and she lifted herself to meet his lips, gasping as his mouth found soft mounds and hard peaks and devoured them. Her nails dug into his upper arms and a tiny moan escaped her throat.

"Shhh," he silenced. "You'll have to be quiet, darling, or we'll wake Margaret."

"It's so sweet," she tried to explain through trembling lips as she stared up at him with her heart in her eyes. "Oh, so sweet, I can hardly bear it . . ."

"I know." He slid down beside her and let

his hand run down her yielding body as his lips touched her eyelids. She whimpered as his mouth moved softly on hers, relishing every tender line of it. "Priss," he breathed. His mouth moved over her flushed face, brushing, exploring, in a rhapsody of taut silence. And all the while his hand roamed over her body, finding the slimness of her legs, the softness of her flat stomach.

Her hands tangled in his thick hair. Her thrusting breasts encountered the hairy roughness of his chest, and she froze. Her eyes opened, wide and soft and full of discovery at the intensity of pleasure the contact gave her.

"Does that please you, little sheila?" he asked softly. He moved, easing his big body over hers. "Don't fight me, all right? I'm only going to let you feel me."

Her lips parted on a rush of breath as he let his weight distribute itself over hers, and she learned something shocking about the differences between men and women. And when his chest melted into hers, she shuddered helplessly, grinding her teeth together and burying her forehead in his throat.

"Delicious," he whispered shakily. "Feeling you . . . this way."

She moved a little, and he groaned.

"Now who's noisy?" she teased with a nervous laugh.

"We'll have to make love in a soundproof

room," he retorted. "Kiss me now. Kiss me hard and slow, and let's get drunk on each other."

His large hands slid under her head and held it while his mouth moved in and took absolute possession of hers. It was like that hot kiss they'd shared back in Australia, and she felt his tongue exploring her mouth.

His body began to move against her, and she let his leg part her own, let him bring their bodies into a shocking kind of intimacy, and cried wildly into his mouth.

"Hush, darling," he whispered. His voice was shaking, and his mouth was insistent. His hands went down to her jeans and began to tug at them.

"Oh, John," she moaned, staring up at him.

"Do you want to?" he asked huskily. His blue eyes were dark and bright and wild-looking. "Do you want me?"

"H . . . h . . . here?" she managed.

He lay there, his body pulsating against hers, his muscles rigid, as he stared into her eyes. "Here?" He blinked and looked down at her and groaned. He forced his body to relax, although the feel of her softness under him wasn't doing his self-control a bit of good. He nuzzled his face against her hair. "I forgot where we were," he said raggedly. "See what you do to me?"

She was learning a lot about that, in a very elemental way. But oddly enough it wasn't embarrassing. It fascinated her to know that he was vulnerable with her.

Her hands moved under his shirt, against the hard muscles of his back, and felt them ripple, as if they liked her hesitant searching. She smiled with pleasure. "I never realized men were so heavy. No . . . !" she protested when he began to lift himself away. "No, I like it, I like feeling you over me."

"God!" he ground out, and shuddered. He rolled over onto his side, taking her with him. He wrapped her against his firm body, holding her there with a heavy leg thrown across hers.

"Sorry," she admitted dryly. "I've got a lot to learn."

"So have I," he confessed. He drew in a steadying breath and brought her small hands to his chest, letting her feel its dampness and rough heartbeat. "I've never had a woman affect me like this."

"I don't believe you."

"No, really," he said, looking into her eyes. He tugged a throw pillow under his head and smiled at her. His fingers brushed her face as they lay together in perfect accord, in a new intimacy. "I've never wanted anyone so much."

She looked down at her fingers against the broad expanse of his chest. Her fingers tugged at his dark body hair. "You're dark here," she noted. "Not blond like on your head."

"Sun doesn't get to my chest often," he reminded her. His eyes studied her pert young breasts pressed into that thickness, and he smiled. His thumbs edged toward the hard peaks and rubbed at them, feeling her shudder. "See how vulnerable we are to each other? You can't be expected to know how rare this kind of thing is. I've lain awake nights ever since you left Providence, aching for you."

Her eyes shot up to his. "But . . ."

"But what?" He brushed the disheveled hair away from her face, and his eyes darkened. "You said you'd write me."

Her eyes fell to his firm mouth. "And you said you'd have your mother write me for you."

He hesitated for a minute. "And you thought . . . yes, I understand now." He rolled onto his back and lifted her over him to study her. "I had this crazy idea that I could keep you at arm's length for another year or two— let this thing between us cool off a bit. Just until you could grow up." He smiled ruefully at her quick frown. "And then when you left, the world went dark for me. I couldn't work for missing you. And you wouldn't even write, you little horror. I looked forward to Easter vacation—I was planning all sorts of reunions. Then you called Renée and said there was a boy . . . !"

She put her fingers over his mouth. "I

chased you unmercifully," she told him. "Everybody remarked about it. I kind of thought you came to see me that last day out of pity. I thought you felt sorry for me and then regretted what had happened and just wanted to forget it."

"I did want to forget," he confessed. "But I couldn't, Priss." His darkening eyes searched down her body to where she was pressed so closely against him, and they clouded perceptibly. "Sit up," he breathed huskily. "Let me look at you, for God's sake!"

Hypnotized, she drew away from him and watched his eyes blaze as they riveted to her.

"You . . . you've been going around . . . with Janie Weeks," she accused softly. The way he was looking at her made her feel faint.

"Janie has nothing at all to do with you and me," he said vaguely. He caught her around the rib cage and brought her breasts down to his mouth. "I kiss you here and taste rose petals," he whispered hungrily, while his mouth nibbled and brushed until she gasped and began to moan helplessly.

He laid her back on the sofa, crushing her mouth under his. One skilled hand cupped, molded, and caressed her, and she wanted him suddenly as she'd wanted nothing else in her life.

He drew away to look at her, and what he saw in her face made him want to throw back his head and scream his frustration. The situation was impossible. He couldn't do it, not on a sofa in someone else's house, not in a flaming rush like this.

Priss watched John deliberate for a long moment and searched his eyes curiously. "John?"

"Marry me," he said.

She trembled all over. Her hands lifted to his face and held it, caressed it. "What?"

"Marry me." He bent and kissed her mouth, softly, tenderly. "Say yes, Priss. Come on. Just one word . . ."

"Yes!" she ground out. Her hands tightened, trying to hold his wandering mouth to hers.

"Not right away," he explained. "I've got . . . a few problems to solve at the station. But by Christmas. Okay?"

"Can I come home with you?" she asked.

"No, darling."

"Why?" she complained.

"Because distance is the only thing that will save your virginity," he said bluntly. "I want you with a disgraceful lust; haven't you noticed?"

"I want you, too."

"Yes. But it has to be done properly," he said heavily. He sat up and tugged her T-shirt back into place. "Once I've had you, Priss, I won't be able to stop; don't you know that?"

"It must be like eating potato chips," she laughed wickedly.

"Much worse," he told her. He smiled slowly. "And once you've had me, you'll want me again. After the first time, anyway."

She felt drunk on pleasure. "I wish we could do it on the beach the first time."

"Pagan," he teased, but his blood was running hot in his veins as he looked down at her slender young body and realized that she wanted him just as much as he wanted her. He could almost picture them, her tanned body writhing under him, her soft young voice moaning with the intensity of pleasure he could arouse . . .

"You can imagine it, can't you?" she asked perceptively. "So can I. Every second of it."

"You don't even know what to expect," he chided.

"Yes, I do." She sat up, too, staring into his eyes. "I'm not that naive. I know exactly what you'll do to me, and how. And I'll bite you, and wrap my legs around you, and move my body . . ."

His mouth hit hers with the force of a tidal wave. He crushed her down into the sofa, his body moving roughly on hers, and she reacted like any woman in love. Her body ached for his, to know it. Her eyes misted with tears as she struggled to make him lose control, to give her what her body was starving for.

But he wasn't a boy, and he could see all too clearly what the consequences would be. Despite the raging desire that consumed him, he tore his body away from hers and rolled onto his back, dragging in air.

"John," she moaned.

He pulled her close against his side and smoothed her long unruly hair. "Close your eyes. It passes. Remember?" he added roguishly.

She blushed, smiling back. "That was my fault. I liked having my way with you," she recalled.

"Someday soon, I'll enjoy letting you. But not," he added with mock anger, "when my hands are tied. It's all or nothing with me, Priss, as you should damned well know by now."

She stared up at his face lovingly. "I guess I can wait, if you can."

"We'll struggle through together," he said with a grin. "Now, get up. God knows what Margaret would say if she walked in."

"As a matter of fact, she did say something about not betraying her trust," Priss confessed.

"What an interesting time to tell me," he returned. He pulled her to her feet, putting her wrists behind her back so he could study her young beauty with eyes that couldn't seem to get enough of it. "Lovely Priscilla," he said finally. "I'll never tire of looking at you. You're beaut."

The deep slow drawl made her tingle. She smiled at him, a woman so completely in love that happiness radiated from every pore of her skin. "So are you."

He breathed deliberately, forcing his heart to behave. "Go to bed," he ordered, bending to kiss her delicately on the mouth. "We'll talk some more in the morning, when it's safer."

Her eyes searched his. "Can't I sleep with you?"

His jaw tensed. "No."

"Just sleep," she pleaded.

He put her away from him with a curt laugh. "I can see that. Sleeping, with you in my arms."

Her eyebrows rose. "Couldn't you?"

He glanced down at her with impatient amusement. "You are a green one, aren't you? No, darling, I couldn't. I want you." At her confused stare, he drew her against his powerful body and deliberately moved her lips against his. "Want," he emphasized even as her mind made the connection between the changed contours of his body and the words.

"Oh," she exclaimed softly.

His shadowy eyes surveyed hers. "Didn't you understand?" he asked gently. "It's uncomfortable for a man."

Her face flushed with color as she met his gaze. "I'm sorry. I really do have a lot to learn."

"It will be fascinating," he murmured, watching her draw discreetly away.

"What will?"

"Shocking you speechless on our wedding night," he said with a wicked grin. "I'll live on the very thought for the next few months."

"John Sterling! And I thought you were a gentleman."

"Remind me, after we're married, to give you the real definition of that word: it's an eye-opener."

"Do I have to go?" she protested.

His bright eyes twinkled. "Unless you want to be attacked."

She sidestepped his playful grab, laughing, bubbling with joy, gloriously beautiful with her pale blonde hair curling around her shoulders in a cloud, and her emerald eyes challenging him from the perfect oval of her lovely face.

"I'll go," she said. "It must be the tropical air getting to your brain."

"It's more a case of you getting to my body," he taunted, his eyes sparkling.

She forced her legs to carry her to the door, and turned back to stare at him, at the thick blond-streaked brown hair her fingers had mussed, at the sensuous look of him with his shirt unbuttoned, his mouth faintly swollen, his eyes glittering with desire.

"I'll be the best wife you ever imagined," she said softly. "I'll love you and give you children, and never even complain when you track mud onto my clean carpets." She grinned. "And in bed, once you teach me how, I'll just blow your mind, Jonathan Sterling."

He smiled slowly. "I can hardly wait."

"Sweet dreams . . . darling," she added, feeling wildly adult and passionate and loved. He hadn't said the words, but he must feel them. She was sure that he did. Otherwise why would he want to marry her when he'd always clung to his freedom? When he smiled back at her, all the tiny doubts rushed away in a surge of wonder, and she danced out the door and into bed, humming a love song under her breath.

The next morning he was sitting at the breakfast table with Margaret when Priscilla got downstairs. She'd overslept and it was midmorning, and she looked as flustered as she felt.

"It's about time," John said with a grimace. "Some way for a newly engaged woman to behave, I'll tell you."

Margaret was grinning from ear to ear. "I'll leave you two to discuss your future alone, while I call Renée and Adam and just burst with pride."

John and Priss laughed as she retreated in a bustle.

"Mom will have it all over the valley before you get back," Priss warned him. "Perhaps you'd better call your mother . . ."

"I told Mother before I left Australia," he said softly. "She was thrilled at my excellent taste in women. Come here, for God's sake!"

She settled down in his lap and smiled into his amused eyes. "I like this a lot," she told him, teasing his mouth with hers. "And I am going to love," she kissed him again, "getting my hands," she bit at his lower lip, "on your body . . . !"

He was kissing her hard, and her head went back under the pressure. She clung to him, trying to be what he wanted, trying to meet his passion with her own.

"When will you learn," he murmured breathlessly, "that I like your mouth open when we kiss?"

"Oh," she whispered back, shaken. She parted her lips and touched them to his. "Like this?"

"Yes . . ."

She felt the penetrating warmth of his tongue, deeply searching, arousing, and she began to ache in the oddest places. Her nails clawed into the big muscles of his upper arms as he held her tight against him.

"Why do you wear these things," he groaned, searching under her T-shirt and finding a lacy little wisp of fabric in his way.

"Take it off if you don't like it," she laughed.

"With Margaret a few steps away?" He chuckled, but his voice was unsteady. He lifted his shaggy head and stared into her eyes warmly. "I'd much prefer your breasts to scrambled eggs, if you want to know."

She blushed from her cheeks down to her throat, and he watched with unholy amusement. "How old did you say you were?" he provoked.

"Almost nineteen," she returned with a flash of spirit. "And just be conceited, while you can. Someday I'll be shocking you!"

"I don't doubt it a bit," he agreed, smiling as he kissed her again, but softly this time. His hand pressed over her breast, and it was warm and strong even through the fabric. "I like stroking you here," he whispered, moving his fingers slowly, erotically.

Her lips opened as she struggled for breath. She looked into his dark hard face with awe. "I like it, too. Your hands . . . are so big."

"You're not big at all," he said gently. "You're delicate and soft and you always smell of gardenias. I don't think I'll ever tire of making love to you."

"I can just see you doing that while you herd cattle," she laughed unsteadily.

"Mustering," he corrected. "In Australia, we muster mobs of cattle."

"In America, we have laws against the mob, and we punch cattle. And we have ranches, not stations. And—"

"And you talk a lot." He stoped her banter

with his lips. "Slide that little hand inside my shirt, and touch me the way I'm touching you. I like being stroked, too."

"Really?" she breathed, all eyes.

"Really."

She'd gotten the first two buttons undone when footsteps sounded in the hall and she groaned. "Oh, damn, just when I'm getting the hang of it . . ."

"Not my fault." He laughed softly, letting her get to her feet. "You should have hurried."

"Just you wait," she threatened as she straightened her T-shirt.

"I'll try," he sighed, studying her slender lovely body. "But I'll ache in the damndest places until then."

She turned away, blushing wildly, as Margaret came back into the room, beaming, full of news from home, the biggest part of it being how thrilled Renée and Adam were about the engagement. And once she started, John and Priss didn't have a chance for further conversation.

Before she knew it, it was time to go with John to the airport. He seemed as reluctant as she felt, and he clung warmly to her hand in the cab and through the terminal. She stopped when he reached Customs and Immigration, and her eyes blurred with tears as she looked up into the rough, broad face she loved so much.

"Don't look like that, or I won't be able to

leave you," he breathed. "God, Priss, I'd give anything to take you with me!"

"Would I fit in your pocket?"

"Not quite, I'm afraid." He pulled her against him. "Although without your high heels, you barely come to my chin."

"John," she said, scanning his face, "you meant it, didn't you? You do want to marry me?"

"Would I have asked you, if I didn't?" he mocked. "After all," he added, bending to whisper, "I haven't seduced you, and we don't have to rush to the altar before your waistline expands, do we?"

She reddened and grinned at him. "I thought about it last night," she confessed. "I thought about taking my clothes off and climbing into bed with you."

"What stopped you?" he asked.

She shrugged, staring at the gray vest of his suit. "I was afraid you might not like being seduced."

He tilted up her chin. "I find the idea wildly exciting," he confided, holding her gaze. "I'd like letting you make love to me."

"Oh, John," she wailed helplessly.

"Too late now," he chuckled.

Her lips smoothed over his, and he stopped laughing and kissed her with hungry passion. His arms crushed her, and his mouth devoured, penetrating, arousing, and she stood there and let him do what he wanted, drowning in the love she felt for him, loving his ardor. Her arms clung around his neck, and she felt her legs tremble when he lifted his head.

"Want me, Priss?" he whispered unsteadily, with blazing eyes. "I want you, too."

"Yes, I can feel . . . I mean . . ." she faltered, drawing away a little in embarrassment.

"We're going to be married," he said softly. "It's all right if we know intimate things about each other now."

She swallowed. "Yes."

He brushed his lips over her closed eyelids. "When we're together again," he whispered, "we'll undress each other and lie together and make out like crazy. I'll try to get back next month, or maybe you can come home."

Her heart was beating so wildly, it hurt her. She buried her face against him, trembling with frustrated ardor. "Could we do that," she questioned unsteadily, "and not go all the way?"

"Yes, I think so," he responded. He drew her close, holding her in a warm embrace, his face against her hair. "I want to do this right. I don't want to anticipate our wedding night, but there are other paths to fulfillment besides the obvious one, little innocent," he whispered softly. "I'll teach you some of them. . . ."

"John," she moaned, clenching her teeth as the wanting became suddenly unbearable.

"Soon, darling," he assured her. He hugged her bruisingly close, and his mouth searched for hers. He kissed her hotly for a long time, and his face was ruddy with frustration when he finally drew away. His nostrils flared as he observed her bright eyes. "Wait for me," he said curtly. "No more dates with the college boy."

"No more," she promised. She smiled slowly. "No more dates for you, either."

"Fat chance," he chuckled. "Every woman I see looks like you these days. Be good, love."

"You, too."

He winked and turned to walk away. She lifted a hand toward him, wanting to call out, wanting to say, I love you. But she didn't. She watched his tall broad-shouldered back until he was out of sight. And then she went back to Margaret's, torn between joy and grief. The waiting was going to be horrible. She didn't know how she could survive it, now that he was going to be hers, at last.

John. Her husband. The thought would sustain her, like water to a desert survivor. She imagined them together in bed, straining against each other in the darkness, loving each other with their bodies. She imagined them with children, John carrying a little boy on his shoulders and laughing. She imagined them being together in the evenings, sitting together while he worked on the books and she graded papers. The dreams were beautiful. And the memories of how it had been between them physically were as satisfying as the dreams.

Chapter Five

*P*riss couldn't remember a time in her life when she'd been so happy. The hidden photograph in her wallet came out of hiding. She showed it to Ronald—to all her friends—with such radiant love and pride that she glowed like a new penny. John was hers at last. Hers!

She rushed downtown to an exclusive department store, where Margaret had an account, and searched for hours until she found just the wedding gown she wanted. It was a dream of a gown, with a keyhole neckline and yards of lace and satin and a floor-length veil. She sighed over it as the saleslady smilingly put it away in a box. Priss could just see how she'd look walking down the aisle to John in it.

She came back to Margaret's house with

stars in her eyes. "You don't mind that I used your card, do you?" Priss asked belatedly when Aunt Margaret seemed hesitant.

"No, darling, of course not," Margaret said gently. "It's just that . . . well, don't you think it might be better to wait a bit on the gown? Just until you and John set a definite date?"

Priss felt a tension in the air. She studied the older woman quietly, intently. "Aunt Margaret, you don't think he'll back out?"

Margaret looked hunted. She sat on the edge of her elegant Chippendale chair with her dainty hands clenched in her lap, her eyes troubled. "Darling, it's been well over a week since John left."

Priss laughed, relieved. "Oh, you mean he hasn't called! I didn't really expect him to, you know. He said he had some things to iron out back home. Selling cattle again, I'll bet; you know how he likes those sales!"

But the older woman didn't laugh. She didn't want to tell Priss what she'd heard when she talked to Renée the previous night. That John had vanished from sight the past few days, and that no one had seen or heard from him. Perhaps it was nothing, but Priss was so caught up in the excitement of the hurried engagement that Margaret was worried. If anything went wrong . . .

"It's just not good to tempt fate," Margaret said finally. "You're so impulsive, darling."

"Stop worrying," Priss chided. She got up

and kissed Margaret's wrinkled cheek. "Everything will be fine. And I'll pay you something every week out of my allowance for the dress," she added softly.

"It's not the money," Margaret denied. She touched Priss's shoulder affectionately. "I'll make you a wedding present of it. I just don't want you to get hurt."

Cold chills worked their way down Priss's backbone, but she hid her anxiety well. "Now stop that," she said. "John would never let me down. He wouldn't have proposed unless he meant it; unless he loved me. Now let's have some lunch. I'm starved!"

Margaret's eyes followed the graceful movement as Priss ran off toward the kitchen. Priss was such a child. She didn't realize that often men thought with their glands more than with their brains. John's hunger for Priss had been obvious, but Margaret wondered if it would fade with his absence from her. Perhaps he had just gotten caught up in Priss's infatuation and had been trapped by his own desire for her. He might even now be looking for a way out of the engagement. That could very well be why he hadn't contacted Priss. It was a disturbing thought, and Margaret was afraid for her niece if it was true.

Meanwhile the seed of suspicion had been firmly planted in Priss's mind, and it didn't go away. When the days kept passing without word from John, she began to worry even more. And finally, just to ease her own silly suspicions, she gave in and called him. She had to be sure. Her grades were falling from the devastating effect of loving him. And even if she went back to Australia to marry him, she had every intention of finishing her education and getting her teaching degree.

She waited until night, when the rates would be cheaper, and let the phone ring for a long time before he finally answered.

"John?" she asked hesitantly.

"Priss!" There was a long static pause. "Priscilla?"

"Yes, it's me," she confirmed. She sat down in the chair beside the hall phone, gripping the receiver. Something was wrong—she could feel it. "John, are you okay?"

She heard a snap and a click, like a lighter firing up. "I'm okay," he said quietly. "How about you?"

"I just miss you, that's all," she said. "I thought you'd call."

"I was going to, later tonight."

She stared at the cord. "How are things going over there?"

There was another pause. "Fine," he said curtly.

"That's nice. How's your mother?"

He sighed heavily. "She's . . . doing very well. She's gone to stay with her sister in California."

"California? She'll enjoy visiting there."

"Yes." He sounded exhausted.

"How are you managing alone?" she teased. There was a pause again. "I'm . . . not alone."

"Are Randolph and Latrice visiting? I heard they had twins a year ago. Your brother must have his hands full," she said softly. She knew Randy and Latrice quite well. They were frequent visitors at the Sterling Run.

"It isn't Randy." There was a thud, as if he'd hit something. "I've got a woman here, if you want to know."

It was like being struck between the eyes with a hammer. The word echoed around in her head, ricocheting wildly. "A . . . cleaning woman?"

He laughed coldly. "Now, you know better than that, don't you?" he asked. "You said yourself, I'm passionate. And being around you was enough to drive any red-blooded man wild. I came back here aching like a boy, and Janie invited me over for dinner . . ." She heard the sigh. "Well, honey, you know what a dish she is. I couldn't help myself. And afterward I asked her to move in."

Janie? Her eyes widened. Janie Weeks, the divorcée he'd been seen with before he flew to Hawaii? He'd said his seeing Janie didn't concern her, but he'd never denied it. And he hadn't spoken of love, either. Only of desire.

She stared at the wall blankly. Her life was ending. John was telling her that he didn't love her. They weren't going to get married and live happily ever after. It had all been a bad joke. It was over.

"But . . . I bought a wedding gown," she began slowly, uncomprehending.

"I came to my senses in time, thank God," he replied stonily. "Priss, you're eighteen years old. Eighteen! I'm twenty-eight. Those ten years, and your innocence, make it all impossible. I need someone older, more sophisticated, more experienced. I can't tie myself down to a kid."

Her body felt washed in heat. He hadn't treated her like a kid. She almost reminded him of that, but her pride wouldn't let her.

"I'm sorry, Priss," he said when she didn't answer. "Really damned sorry. But you have to understand, I went off the beam for a while. You went to my head a little, and I got some strange ideas about the future. Now I'm back in my right mind and stone sober, and I want my freedom more than I want you. It wouldn't have worked out. Priss, are you there?"

"I'm here." She sounded almost normal, despite the fact that her heart was breaking and there were tears in her eyes. "I hear you."

There was another pause. "You understand, surely," he said roughly. "If you'd been a little older or more experienced, we could have had a good time together, with no strings. But you're just too intense, Priss. And worlds too

young for me. My oath, I shudder just thinking about what marriage would have been
like with you."

Her lips trembled, and the tears overflowed.
"I love you," she whispered brokenly. "How
do I stop?"

He swallowed, and she heard a ragged
breath over the phone. "Priss," he ground out.
"It's just desire, nothing more," he said, but
he sounded odd. "The same desire I felt for
you. But I'm over mine, and you'll get over
yours. For God's sake, you didn't really expect
me to marry you just so I could sleep with
you?"

The way he said it made her sound like a
naive little idiot. She took a steadying breath.
"That's me, all right," she laughed bitterly.
"I'm just a kid, after all. Just a green little
girl . . ."

"Isn't it better to find out now than after
we'd married and messed up our lives?" he
growled. "You're well rid of me. Just think of
it that way, can't you?"

"I'll do my best; I promise you," she said,
hating him. "After all, I'm young. And Ronald
won't let me pine away."

There was a pause before he spoke. "Your
life is your own concern and none of mine.
I've got Janie. And my God, what a contrast
she is to you," he added on a cold laugh. "All
woman. Sweet and wild and giving, not a

child looking for rainbows. She's satisfied with plain sex, and I don't have to buy her a wedding band."

She could picture him with the woman. She could see them. . . . She closed her eyes, aware of a tension on the other end of the line, but it didn't register. "So that's that," she said quietly. "What a good thing you didn't get me a ring. I'm only sorry you didn't come to your senses before I went out and told the whole world we were getting married."

"Gossip dies down eventually." He sounded bored.

"For men, certainly," she replied. "Not for women. Especially not here."

"Well, then, you'll just have to keep your little chin up, won't you?" he informed her. "Tell them you dropped me—I don't mind."

She drew in a deep breath while her heart seemed to go crazy. "Lie to my friends the way you lied to me? No, thanks. I still have some integrity," she said with bitter pride. "I'm glad you came to your senses, John," she added on a broken sob. "I wouldn't marry you now if you were—"

"You wouldn't be asked," he interrupted coldly. "I want a woman, not a silly little girl. At least now you won't be following me around like a pet dog anymore, will you?"

Tears burst from her eyes. She felt sick and empty and dead inside. "No," she cried. "I won't."

There was a brief silence on the other end of the line. But she hung up quietly before he had the chance to say anything else. She couldn't have borne another word.

She cried and cried, the tears silent and hot and profuse. She was still sitting there when Margaret came into the hall and stopped suddenly.

"Priscilla! What is it, dear?" she asked, concerned.

"That was John," Priss whispered, red-eyed. "He isn't going to marry me. He's decided that his divorcée is more than enough for him. He can have her without marriage, you see."

Margaret caught her breath. "Can he, now?" she said gruffly. "Here, I'll call Renée, and we'll find out what's going on."

Renée answered the phone when Margaret called, her own eyes red, her voice wobbling as she told Margaret it was all true, that John did . . . have a woman at his house, that he'd been to see them, to tell them about why he was ending the engagement.

"Can she talk to me, Margaret?" Renée asked Adam's sister.

"No," Margaret said. "She's gone up to her room in tears. She's just devastated. Why, Renée? Why would he do such a thing?"

Renée had to fight for control. "Priss is young, she'll . . . get over it. Darling, tell her to call me when she's calmer, will you? And thank you, Margaret, for taking such . . . such good care of her."

"Renée, are you all right? You sound odd . . ."

"I've got a cold," she replied. "I'm fine. Look after Priss. And yourself. 'Bye, darling."

She hung up, wiping the tears away. Adam came into the living room and took her quietly into his arms.

"Poor Priss," she muttered tearfully.

"Yes," he agreed, patting her. "But John was right. With the situation as it was, what else could he do?"

"What a burden he placed on us, though, darling," she stated despondently.

"A horrible mess, all around," Adam agreed. He smoothed her hair. "At least we can spare Priss." Adam kissed her. "Regrets aren't going to do either of them any good. Besides, Priss is young, as we keep saying. The young heal quickly."

"I hope you're right," Renée said fervently. "Oh, I do hope you are."

It was all Priss could do to lie in bed that night. She couldn't call her parents back. She couldn't bear the sympathy she knew would be in their voices. Margaret seemed to understand that because she left her niece alone after bringing her a cup of tea and two aspirin to help her sleep.

The next morning Priss slept late. It had been long past midnight when she finally dropped off to sleep the night before. She got up, dressed in jeans and a neat top and sneakers, and went downtown.

The lady who'd waited on her in the department store didn't ask any questions as she brought out the dress Priss had watched her put away so carefully. She arranged the ticket to credit Margaret's account, and all the while Priss stared blankly at the gown.

It was white satin with alençon lace and illusion lace appliqués from its keyhole neckline to the empire waist. It had puffy little sleeves and a Juliet cap with a full veil flowing from it. Priss had never seen anything so exquisite in all her life. She remembered daydreaming, just days before, about how it would feel to have John see her in it, as they stood before a minister and pledged to love each other forever.

"Here we go," the saleslady said politely, getting Priss to sign the credit slip. "I'm sorry things didn't work out."

"So am I," Priss said in a ghost of a voice.

The saleslady's polite smile faded. "Time helps," she said quietly, and her eyes hinted at a past hurt that must have been similar to Priss's. "There are kind, wonderful men in this world. I found mine on the second try. Don't give up."

Priss found a smile for her, for that tiny bit of understanding that eased her path. "Thank you," she said, and with one last lingering look at the gown, she turned and walked out of the store.

She didn't go to class that day. Instead she wandered through a tourist attraction, one of the many botanical gardens that Honolulu was famous for. Her eyes drank in orchids of every species, and oleander and birds of paradise and candle flowers. She touched the blooming fronds of the exquisite orange-blossomed flame tree, the royal poinciana, and sniffed the perfume that was much sweeter than anything in a bottle.

Eventually she sat down on a bench and let the numbness creep over her, deaden the pain. It was a matter of making it through one day at a time, she told herself. First she had to forget John. She had to forget the day she'd left Australia, and the night he'd flown to Honolulu. She had to remember that John wanted a woman, not a little girl, and that she wasn't worth a wedding ring to him.

She listened to her own self-pity and laughed out loud. No, that wasn't her thing. She wouldn't be caught in that bitter trap. She'd have to get her mind on something else, and fast.

Without really thinking about where she was going, she walked into the city hospital, to the admissions desk, and asked for the personnel office. And then she went in and volunteered some free time.

Inevitably people asked about her engagement, and she repeated again and again the pat little speech she had devised. It wasn't the lie John had suggested, but it wasn't the truth, either. She and John had decided that her education came first, she explained to save her savaged pride. It was much too soon for marriage. But there were sly smiles and knowing looks, and she knew she wasn't fooling anyone—least of all herself. Over and over she kept hearing John's deep voice telling her what a silly little girl she was. Laughing at her for following him around "like a little pet dog." Her pride was shattered. Despite the healing powers of time, the humiliation lingered. She should have realized that all he'd wanted was her body. She should have known it would never work out. If only she could stop loving him!

The nights were the roughest. Her days were full now: When she wasn't in class, she was working in the children's ward, reading stories and straightening pillows and making little faces smile. By helping other people, she forgot her own problems and turned outward instead of inward. But at night the memories returned in full force, dark and sweet. John, holding her. John, touching her responsive young body. John, promising heaven after they were married. He haunted her like a persistent ghost, and she knew all too well that it was more than she could bear to go back to Providence anytime soon to visit.

She talked to her mother about it eventually, because it worried her so much.

"I'm not a coward, really I'm not," she told Renée. "It's just that it still hurts, and . . ."

"I know, darling," Renée said. She had to bite her tongue not to blurt out the whole horrible story. But Adam was right, it wouldn't help things. "Suppose Dad and I fly over and see you?"

She smiled. "That would be nice, but can you afford it?"

"Darling, Margaret browbeat your father into accepting the fare as an anniversary present. How about that?"

"I love Aunt Margaret!"

"So do we. We'll talk more about the visit later. But getting back to you, how are you, darling?"

Priss managed not to tell the truth. "I'm doing fine. I'm working in a children's ward, and I think I've got a secretarial job lined up for summer vacation. I wish I could come home, but . . ."

"Yes, I know. It's too soon," Renée sighed. "It would be terribly awkward if you ran into John."

"Have . . . have you seen him?" she asked, hating the question because it betrayed her.

Renée had to grit her teeth. Oh, yes, she'd seen the poor miserable soul, looking years past his true age, his eyes so haunted that she couldn't look into them.

"Actually, no, darling," Renée lied while tears welled up in her eyes.

"Oh." Priss sighed. "Well, I suppose it's all for the best. Ronald and I are going to see that new comedy movie tonight. It should be fun."

"You aren't still grieving?" her mother asked tentatively.

"Of course not," Priss assured her. "I'm getting along just fine. Perhaps it was infatuation after all."

Renée bit her tongue. "Perhaps it was. Take care, darling. I love you. Dad sends his love, too."

"That works both ways," Priss said softly. "Thanks for being such great parents. I'll call you again soon."

"Yes, please do. 'Bye."

Priss hung up and closed her eyes on fresh tears. Someday it would stop hurting. Someday she'd forget. Someday, somehow, the images would fade and there would be another spring, another season of love. . . .

Chapter Six

𝒥t was almost dark by the time Renée and Adam Johnson pulled up in front of their small bungalow and caught sight of Priss.

"Darling, how lovely you look," Renée called out as her daughter ran across the paddock and into her arms. "College has made a sophisticate out of you."

"I'll say," Adam agreed, slamming the car door. He kissed Priss warmly. It had been more than four years since his daughter had been home, and trips to Hawaii had necessarily been infrequent. He was looking forward to getting to know Priss all over again. "What a lady we raised!"

"Soon to be unrecognizable as I begin

teaching primary school," she bantered. "I can hardly wait. I brought back some storybooks from Honolulu for the children, just in case I couldn't get them locally."

"And I baked an apple pie, just for you, darling," Renée told her, putting a motherly arm around her daughter's shoulders.

"I know," Priss grinned. "I smelled it when I walked into the house. How was the luncheon?"

"Lovely," Renée said. "We went home with Betty Gaines and spent the rest of the day planning your homecoming party," she added with a smile. "That's why we couldn't meet you. Uh, John said he didn't mind giving you a ride."

Priss's face clouded. "No, he didn't."

Renée started to speak, but Adam shook his head quickly. "Betty Gaines teaches third grade now. You remember her, don't you?" Adam asked.

"Yes, of course," she replied warmly. "I liked her very much. It's so sweet of her to give me a party."

"Well, come on," Renée urged. "Let's go inside, darling. It's so good to have you home!"

"I'll miss Aunt Margaret a bit," Priss confided. "She was such fun to live with!"

"She'll miss you, I'm sure," Renée said. She led the way into the kitchen, where Priss and

Adam sat down while she made coffee and thick ham sandwiches. "By the way, how about Ronald George? He's taking a position here, too, isn't he?"

Priss grinned. "He says so, for a little while, anyway, until he proves to his father that he can make his own living without waiting to inherit the family fortune. But just between us, I think he'll end up back in England eventually."

"He's a fine young man," said Adam, who had met Ronald during his visits to Hawaii. He glanced at Priss. "We thought you might marry him."

"Ronald?" Her expression made clear her feelings for the man in question. "No, he's a lot of fun and we're great friends. But we don't even think alike on the important issues."

Renée's eyes closed briefly, but she didn't say anything else.

"I'm glad you wanted to come back here to teach," Adam said with quiet pride. "I'm sure you could have made a bigger salary in Hawaii."

"But my parents aren't in Hawaii," she retorted. "I was getting sort of homesick, to tell the truth."

They all laughed, and afterward things settled down into a normal, sweetly familiar routine. By bedtime, Priss felt as if she'd never been away. Except when she started remembering John. Sleeping in her bed again was an ordeal, because it held such powerful memories. She imagined that she could still feel the weight of his body above hers, feel the hard, warm crush of his mouth. And it was hours before she finally coaxed her mind into sleep. But when she slept, it was dreamlessly for once.

The primary school in Providence was a small brick building and nothing fancy to look at, but her few students were enthusiastic and attentive, and she loved working with them. And although they missed the teacher they'd begun the year with, they quickly warmed to Priss. First-graders, she thought, were the best kind of people to be around. Except for the twins . . .

The twins, Bobby and Gerry, were all that John had hinted, and more. Apparently they had very little discipline or attention at home, Priss noted, because they did everything possible to attract any kind of notice from the other students. On her first day in class, they put frogs in her desk and hid the chalk and nailed her chair to the floor. She sent a note home to Randy and Latrice to be signed, but the next day the boys came back empty-handed.

"Gerry, where is the note I sent home with

you?" she asked one of the twins, the one whose hair was a deeper red than his brother's.

"Uh, we lost it," he said and smirked.

"Dead right, we did," Bobby agreed. "Wind got it."

She pursed her lips. "Really?" she asked.

They grinned at her. "Fair dinkum!" they promised.

"I'll get you another one to take home this afternoon," she said, then thought better of the idea. "No, tell you what, I'm going to a party tomorrow night. Your parents will be there, so I'll give it to them myself and save you boys the trouble."

Their expressions were comical. They began protesting at once, but she held up a hand and began the lesson. It was the first of many skirmishes to come.

The brightest spot in the week was the arrival of Ronald George, who was helping out in Betty Gaines's third grade. His twinkling wit helped to pass the time, and Priss was grateful for a familiar face other than her father's among the staff. She still had lunch with Adam, though, and she noticed that Ronald got into the habit of sitting with Amanda Neal, one of the other teachers. He grinned at Priss sheepishly, and she winked back. Mandy was very pretty, petite, blonde, and blue-eyed. And very British. That, she told herself, looked like the beginning of a nice match.

Friday ended with a bang, as the twins beat up another boy, whose mother came to violently protest her son's abuse by "those ruffians!" Priss calmed her at great length and hurried home to eat her supper before it was time to dress for the party.

As she ate she tried to control the butterflies in her stomach. It was going to be a good night, she told herself. She was going to glow as she never had in the old days; she was going to bring John Sterling to his knees! Let him see what he was missing, what he'd thrown away. Her heart lifted as she contemplated her old vision of floating down an elegant staircase to watch his jaw fall, his eyes burn with wanting her. She smiled to herself. Yes, that would be sweet, to see his desire for her and show him that she felt nothing at all.

"I have to talk to Randy and Latrice about the twins," she told her parents as she finished her second cup of coffee. "They beat up Mrs. Morrison's boy today."

Adam nodded. "The boy's something of a bully, but they shouldn't have ganged up on him," he agreed. "I suppose Randy and Latrice will come to the party. If Latrice is home. She travels so much these days."

"For pleasure?" Priss asked.

"I suppose. I don't think she and Randy get

along very well. And John can't be making it easy for them," he said quietly. "He's been pure hell, from what I hear. He's very bitter."

About what? Priss wondered, but only nodded. "Will John be at the party?"

"I don't know," he replied. "He's rarely seen these days. He sticks to the station like glue, except for an occasional trip to cattle sales."

That didn't sound like the old John, who had loved people and socializing. She stared at her father. "Are things bad at the station?" she probed.

"They have been," he said vaguely. "Drought, you know. But I guess they're picking up now. John just bought that new Ford."

"It's not a luxury car, but it's nice just the same," Renée interrupted. "We'd better rush, darlings."

Upstairs she put on the long white gown with its one shoulder strap and side slits and sequined bodice and studied herself in the mirror. She'd filled out in five years. She still wasn't quite voluptuous, but she wasn't thin, either. She looked good, she told herself. She put on a pearl necklace and bracelet and ear studs, and a minimum of makeup. To top it all off, she draped a blue fox boa around her neck. Yes, she thought. Yes, that would be just the thing to parade in front of John Sterling.

When she went back downstairs, her parents were waiting for her. Her father was dressed in dark evening clothes; her mother in a royal blue gown.

"Gorgeous couple." Priss beamed. "You look lovely. You, too, Dad."

"I'll box your ears," he threatened. "You're a dish yourself. Didn't we do well?" he teased Renée.

"Yes, we did, darling." Renée grinned, taking his arm. "You'll wow 'em, sweetheart," she told her daughter.

Priss fiddled with the boa. "I'd like to stop by the Sterling place on the way to the party, if you don't mind," she said quietly. "I need to speak to Randy and Latrice alone, and even if they do come to the party, I realize it would be better to see them in a quieter setting."

"No problem," Adam said. "Shall we go, ladies?"

It was a chilly night, and Priss almost wished she'd worn a jacket instead of the boa. But the car soon warmed up, and it didn't take long to wind up the oleander-lined driveway at the Sterling station to the old Colonial-style house with its graceful porches. It had been recently repainted and gleamed like a stoic ghost among the gum and wattle trees.

"I'll only be a minute," Priss promised. She got out of the car and walked slowly up the steps onto the wide porch. It looked just as it had years ago, when she used to come up here and have lunch with John's mother. She'd always loved the elegance of the old house.

She knocked on the door, fraught with nerves, wondering who would answer it. Footsteps sounded, and the door was thrown open. But it wasn't John, it was Randy.

He was shorter than his brother, with reddish-brown hair and pale blue eyes, and in his younger days he had had a frightful superiority complex. But now he seemed different as he grinned at Priss and let her into the house.

"Well, hello," he greeted deeply, his eyes clearly approving little Priscilla Johnson's new look. "Priscilla, how you've grown up!" He admired her.

"One does, inevitably," she said and smiled back. She was trembling, but she maintained her poise. Was John nearby; was he here? she wondered feverishly.

"Can I help you?" he asked, looking puzzled as to why she might be there.

"Yes. I need to speak with you and Latrice, about the twins," she said gently. "I'm sorry to bother you at home like this, but I sent a note, and it got lost. And at the party, it would be impossible. It won't take long, I promise."

"The twins," he said with a resigned sigh. "I've thought of tying them to trees, you know. They ignore me and laugh at Latrice—when she's home," he added darkly.

"What's all the commotion?" came a deep familiar drawl from the living room doorway. It was John, of course.

Tonight he was wearing close-fitting tan slacks and a brown plaid jacket with a white shirt and tie. Powerful muscles strained at the garments as if they were purchased when he was a little lighter, less mature. He looked faintly rumpled, and her eyes went over his worn garments with faint hauteur.

His cutting eyes flashed angrily as he received that insult, and they lingered on her own attire. If she'd expected to bring him to his knees, she was immediately disappointed. He eyed her indifferently, and then turned away. "I'm going on over to the Gaineses'," he told his brother. "See you there; but I'm not staying long. Parties aren't my style these days," he added with a cold smile in Priss's direction. By the way, honey," he drawled, "we're simple folk around here. Designer gowns aren't the routine. All they accomplish is to make the other women who can't afford them feel uncomfortable."

Her eyes narrowed. "Yes, I can see the current style doesn't owe anything to fashion," she added with another meaningful glance at his own clothing. "You'll have to forgive me. I grew used to genteel company in Hawaii."

"Like that pommy you brought back?" John taunted with cold eyes and a cutting smile.

"At least," she replied carelessly, "he has excellent breeding and rather admirable taste in suits!"

John's face stiffened. He nodded toward Randy and walked out the door without a backward glance.

Randy looked as if he would have loved to say something, but he only shrugged uncomfortably.

"Latrice!" he called up the staircase. "Could you come down here, please?"

Seconds later an angry sigh came from upstairs, and Latrice descended. She was redheaded and petite, with a kewpie-doll prettiness.

"There you are," Priss said, forcing herself to forget John and his bad temper and get her mind on the present. She smiled. "It's good to see you again, Latrice. I'm afraid my visit isn't purely social, though. I want to have a word with you about the twins."

Latrice laughed huskily. "Oh, my. This sounds serious."

"Not yet. But we're headed that way," Priss said and recounted the incidents of the past two days.

Latrice gasped. "All that, in just two days?"

"I told you they're getting out of hand," Randy told his wife sharply.

She glared at him and seemed to be on the verge of making a sharp retort when Priss interrupted.

"Uh, the twins?" she prompted. They both looked at her. "I barely saved you from a day in court with the Morrison boy's mother," she added meaningfully.

Latrice sighed. "Well, we'll just take their telly away from them for a week," she said. "That should do it."

"Have you looked in their room?" Randy protested. "They've got a million damned toys. Being locked in there without the telly isn't a punishment; it's a reward!"

"Then, we'll restrict their toys as well."

Priss felt uncomfortable. It really wasn't the time to go into child psychology and the attention-getting mechanism that was overly active in the twins.

"What good will that do? They need a good beating," Randy said.

"You will not hit my sons!" Latrice fired right back.

Priss cleared her throat and Latrice looked at her with a guilty smile. "I'm sorry," she mumbled. "We'll have a talk with them, and we'll do . . . something," she added. She smiled politely. "Thank you for bringing it to our attention."

"I didn't like to bother you tonight," Priss replied, "but it was reaching the critical stage."

"That's all right, Priss," Randy said. "If the boys don't improve, we'll want to know about it."

"Yes, I'll see that you do. Well, I'd better

run. I left Mom and Dad out in the car. Are you coming to the party?"

"Of course." Randy grinned, hugging a reluctant Latrice to his side. "We don't get invited out that often these days, do we, darling?"

She glowered at him. "No. Not that often."

Priss mumbled a quick good night and beat a path to the door.

Chapter Seven

ave any luck?" Adam Johnson asked his daughter after she'd climbed into the backseat and he was starting the car.

Priss gave him a rueful smile. "I hope so. They're being deprived of television."

Adam shook his head. "It won't work."

"Stop disillusioning me," Priss said, hitting his shoulder playfully.

"Did you see John?" Renée asked quietly.

Priss sat back. "Yes."

"I don't think he even noticed us," Adam related dryly. "He got straight into his car and drove off in a cloud of dust."

She stared out the window. "How odd," she said tensely, but she didn't say anything else and, after a quickly exchanged look, neither did her parents.

Betty Gaines was a petite woman with salt and pepper hair and a glowing personality. She made them all feel right at home, and Priss was delighted to find a few young people her age at the party.

"What fun this is," Ronald George commented in her ear. "I can hardly wait to go to sleep."

"Hush!" she scolded. "It's a lovely party!"

"Your Aussie friend doesn't seem to think so," he returned, glancing toward John, who was standing alone in the corner with a cup of punch in one hand, glaring at them.

She peeked through her lashes, hoping that John was miserable. Hoping that she'd hurt him. "No, he doesn't," she said too sweetly. "Why don't we go over and cheer him up, darling?" she laughed, and revenge glittered from her eyes. She caught his sleeve and half dragged him across the room.

"Why, hello, John," Priss said with false warmth. "I don't think you've ever met Ronald George, have you? Ronald, this is John Sterling, who owns the property adjoining ours."

"So pleased to meet you, old chap," Ronald said with his easy grin, and extended a hand.

John looked as if he were being offered a piece of moldy bacon. But after a slight hesitation, he shook the hand roughly and let it fall.

"I hear you're in cattle," Ronald nodded politely. "My father has a cow or two." He grinned. "He owns a chain of steak restaurants. You might have heard of them—The George Steak Houses?"

"Sorry," John said brusquely, staring down at the smaller man from his formidable height. He towered over everyone, Priss thought. He was powerfully built, right down to the huge hands whose gentleness she hated to remember.

"Ah, well, not to worry." Ronald began to look uncomfortable. He cleared his throat. "Nice town, Providence."

"My grandfather thought so," John returned quietly. "He founded it."

"Oh. Really?"

"Ronald doesn't know much about Australian history," Priss told John. "But he is quite an authority on financial matters." She smiled vaguely. "He and his father have made a fortune in investments."

John seemed to withdraw. His eyes were the only things alive in that searing face, and they cut into Priss's face. "Have they?"

"We've had some small successes," Ronald said, with a puzzled glance at Priss. He cleared his throat. "Uh, darling, wouldn't you like some punch?" he asked hopefully.

But Priss was enjoying herself. Revenge had a sweet taste, and she was repaying all John's taunts, all his cutting remarks as she played up to Ronald. "Yes, I would," she agreed. "Would you bring me one?"

"Delighted!" Ronald said and hurried away.

"Isn't Ronald a dream?" she sighed, viewing the teacher's thin back with adoring eyes. "I do so admire his taste in clothes. And he has the most delightfully cultured background. He's quite unique in these parts, don't you think?"

"He's a thoroughbred, all right," John said with a cold smile. He gulped down the rest of his punch and put the empty glass on a nearby table before he lit a cigarette. "Why didn't the two of you stay in Hawaii?"

"My family is here," she replied. Her eyes wandered over his hard face, and she saw new lines in it. A twinge of aching grief went darting through her, but she forced herself not to show it. There was no hope that she'd ever kiss that hard mouth again, or know the strength of those arms holding her. She might as well steel herself against lost hope.

"God, you've changed," he said, staring down at her.

"I've only grown up. Aren't you delighted?" she asked with venomous sweetness. "I won't be following you around like a pet puppy from now on."

He stared down at his cigarette and shadows deepened in his eyes. For an instant he looked odd. Strangely haunted. "Yes. I'm delighted." He put the cigarette to his lips and took a long draw from it. "I have to go. We're starting the muster tomorrow, and I'll have a mob of cattle waiting."

"Well, at least you're already wearing your work clothes, aren't you?" she asked with an empty smile. "You'll save some time that way."

His face grew stony. He smiled back, but it was a chilling smile. "There's an old saying about clothes making the man. But out here, little sheila, it's the man who counts. I may not dress to suit your newly acquired sophistication. And I may not have the cultured background of your pet pommy over there. But I'm satisfied with my life. Can you say the same of yours?"

She couldn't, but she smiled though it killed her. "Without you in it, you mean?" she asked coldly. "Oddly enough, I look on the breaking of our engagement as a lucky escape. It forced me to take another look at Ronald." She glanced toward the punch bowl, where he was filling their cups. "My, isn't he gorgeous?"

John smiled ironically. "Just your style, Priscilla," he agreed. His eyes burned her. "Perhaps you're able to satisfy his watered-down passions. You'd never have satisfied mine. Good night."

She stared after him with trembling lips.

Why did he continually do that to her? Why did he say cutting things and walk away before she could come up with a suitable reply? She picked up the cup he'd put on the table and was actually raising it over her head when Ronald came back.

"No!" he burst out, grabbing it. His eyes were incredulous. "You weren't really going to throw it at him?"

"Why not?" she asked abruptly. "Don't be so stuffy!"

Ronald looked toward the door where John had exited. "Poor chap," he sympathized. "You do give him the boot at every opportunity, don't you?"

"He deserves all he gets and more," she stated angrily. She shifted restlessly, her evening ruined. "I wonder why Randy and Latrice haven't shown up?"

"Oh, the other Sterlings?" he asked. "Betty said Latrice had called and explained something about a headache."

"More like a fight," Priss groaned. "And my fault. I had to tell them about the twins, and she and Randy went at it. Oh, what a miserable day!"

"Would you like to leave?" he asked.

"No. I'd like to try not to ruin Betty's evening after all the trouble she's gone to." She forced a smile. "Shall we circulate and pretend to be jubilant?"

He grinned. "Delighted! While we're circulating, could we perhaps circulate in the direction of the gorgeous little blonde?"

"Mandy?" She grinned back, observing the small teacher in the corner all alone. "Yes, let's!"

"How are you getting on with the Sterling twins, by the way?" he asked as they walked toward Mandy.

She sipped her punch. "I'm going to ask for a raise."

"That bad, hmmm? Listen, if we could get their father into the military, I think I could pull enough strings to have him transferred to another commonwealth country . . ."

"He's already served," she said.

"Drat!"

"Randy and Latrice said they'd take care of it," she added, without divulging their recipe for success.

He sighed. "I'll remember you in my prayers, old girl."

"Thanks."

After the party was over and Priss was lying in her own empty bed, she couldn't manage to get to sleep. All she saw was John. Her heart seemed to swell up at just the thought of him. And she'd thought it was over, that she could see him and not be affected. That she hated him. That she could take her revenge and not feel anything. Ha! She'd cut him tonight all right, in many ways. But as sweet as it had been at the time, her conscience hurt her now. He was so different. He looked so much older, and he dressed like someone without much money. But that was impossible: he still had the Run. He and Randy had the Run, she corrected. She frowned. That was another puzzle. Why were Randy and his family living with John? It was all so confusing. And most confusing were her own turbulent emotions. She was shocked to find how vulnerable she still was to John. That would have to be kept carefully concealed. Perhaps if she worked at it, though, she could force her heart to shut him out for good. Perhaps.

She rolled over. She'd realized tonight that she wasn't indifferent to him. And he'd proved to her that whatever he felt, it wasn't regret over the past. He'd said he was quite satisfied with his life.

After all that had happened, why did she ache so from looking at him? Why did her body tremble with desire to feel his again? Why were there tears in her eyes and a pain like rheumatism in her poor heart, if it was all over? She buried her face in the pillow. It was going to take some self-control to stay here. She wondered if she could. . . .

She slept late the next morning and got up just in time to wave good-bye to her parents as they went into Providence to shop for groceries at the tiny store there. She put on an old pair of jeans and a black T-shirt and went out walking.

It was a glorious spring day. The whole outdoors smelled of freshness and new growth, and far away she could hear cattle bawling. It was spring, after all, she reminded herself. They'd be mustering cattle over on the Sterling Run. She stuck her hands into her pockets as she walked, wishing she could go over and watch. The muster was much like an American roundup, with calves being branded and immunized and neutered, and sweating stockmen trying to keep up with the pace set by John, who never seemed to tire. She wondered if Randy helped these days. In the old days, Randy hadn't liked getting dirty.

Her eyes went to the distant peaks of the Great Dividing Range and she smiled at their grandeur against the clear azure sky. She loved Australia; droughts, floods, and all. Summer would soon be here, and with it the Wet, the flooding that she remembered from the days before she went to college. She shuddered a little. The Warrego went out of its banks in flood, and sometimes it was impossible to get across the streams that crisscrossed the bottoms. Flash flooding back in Alabama had been nothing like it was here, where even the lightest rain could make little streams into rivers.

She'd often wished it would flood when she was at John's house in the old days, so that she could have an excuse to spend the night with him and his mother. She wondered how

Mrs. Sterling was liking America, and if she ever planned to come back. Odd that she'd gone so willingly, when she loved this country as much as John did. And Randy hated station life; he was a city boy at heart. What was he doing up here so far from Sydney and his sheep property?

As she walked she caught a glimpse of John in the distance, tall in the saddle, his silver-belly Stetson catching the light as he eased his stockhorse in and out of the small mob of cattle he was driving down the long road between her father's property and the Run.

His head turned, and he seemed to see her. The aboriginal stockman with him herded the cattle along, with the help of one of the station's prize stockdogs, an Australian shepherd.

John turned his horse and rode over to the fence, waiting for Priss to come up to it.

It was like time turning back, she mused, as she walked to meet him. Once, she'd have run. But that would be undignified. Not to mention foolish. Let him think she didn't care anymore.

"Hello," she said. "Scorching cattle today?"

He tilted his hat back. "Something like that." He lifted his dimpled chin and stared at her quietly.

"Was that Little Ben?" she asked, nodding toward the lean young stockman who was riding away from them.

"Yes. You remembered."

"I do have a memory," she reminded him. "How's Big Ben?"

"He hasn't aged a day," he told her. "He's still the best stockman I've got. Billy Riggs is jackerooing for us these days."

She knew Billy from school: he'd been in her senior class. "Yes, I know him. He always wanted to work cattle."

"And you always wanted to teach school," he reminisced, studying her.

"Are you disappointed that I don't wear horn-rimmed glasses and black skirts with white blouses and have my hair in a bun?" she inquired on a mocking laugh. "Schoolteachers are no longer dull and droll and unappealing."

"As I see," he agreed.

She searched him over, her eyes helplessly following the play of muscles under his khaki shirt as he shifted in the saddle. He was perfect physically, the most devastating man she'd ever seen.

"How are you liking the school in Providence?"

"Very much. I'm delighted that they let me take over for Miss Ross while she was having her surgery. It will give me a head start when school begins again in the fall."

"The twins are brooding," he remarked. "I suppose you know they've had their television privileges revoked. To top it all, Randy and

Latrice had one hell of a fight last night and Latrice took off bag and baggage on another trip."

"I'm sorry about that," she responded quietly.

"What those children need is a lot of love and attention—none of which they receive," he uttered regretfully. "Randy is too involved with investments and Latrice in travel. They hardly communicate these days, and they have no time at all for the boys."

"That's sad."

"Yes. If I had sons, they'd be with me as much as possible," he said, and something in his eyes caught her attention. "I've got the twins with me today, watching the muster. They're behaving quite well."

"I'm sure they like being around you," she affirmed. "They're outdoor kids."

"Randy hates the outdoors," he remarked. "Flies, you know."

She smiled involuntarily. "How in the world did he wind up here with you?"

His face changed. "What are *you* doing out here?" he asked, changing the subject.

"Just walking. It's such a lovely day," she said.

He nodded. "I have to get back," he said. He hesitated, his eyes narrowing as they searched her face, and he asked suddenly, "Want to come up behind me?"

He seemed to regret the question almost immediately, but she was too shocked to notice. She remembered aching to have him ask that before she left for Hawaii. She had to admit it now: She wanted to be close to him. In spite of everything, part of her ached for it. But she knew she couldn't be that close without giving herself away completely. She couldn't risk it.

"No, thanks," she said. "I haven't been on a horse in years. It's safer on the ground."

He searched her eyes and smiled mockingly. "You aren't flattering yourself that I had ulterior motives for that invitation?" he taunted. "I was offering you a lift. Nothing more."

Her blood ran hot. She seethed at him with years of bitter hatred in her eyes. "I'd rather hitch a ride with a cobra!" she shot back. "I'm not in the market for an outback cowboy!"

"My bloody oath, you're asking for it," he bit off, and something in his eyes frightened her.

"Not from you," she said coldly. "I want nothing from you. Not ever again."

"Praise God," he returned with a cutting smile.

She whirled and dashed off across the paddock, hardly noticing where she put her feet.

John watched her go with a bleak expression, eyes narrowed in something approaching pain as he followed her lithe figure until it was out of sight. After a minute, he turned his mount with unusual roughness and urged the stockhorse into a gallop, his face as hard as stone.

Priscilla knew there was going to be trouble the minute the twins walked into her classroom Monday morning.

They glared at her horribly and did everything possible to disrupt the class. By lunch, when nothing she said or did worked, she went into the school office and phoned the Sterling Run.

Randy answered, and Priss hardly gave him time to say hello before she poured it all out.

"They have hidden my chalk, they've thrown schoolbooks out the window, they've talked and catcalled and made noise when I was trying to conduct class, and I'm at the end of my rope. Randy, I'm going to have to send them to the principal and let him deal with them, and it may mean expulsion."

"In the first grade," he sighed. "Where have Latrice and I gone wrong? Listen, Priss, I've got a meeting with some out-of-town cattlemen, and I can't get away right now. Latrice stormed out of here Friday night, bag and baggage, and went to Bermuda on another holiday—John and I are half crazy with work . . ."

"I'm sorry you have problems, but I do think this takes priority, Randy," she said with gentle firmness. "Expulsion on the twins' record at this early stage in their education would be devastating. You can see that, can't you?"

He muttered something. "All right, Priss, I'll be there in fifteen minutes."

She went back to the classroom, and as luck would have it, the twins had just returned early from lunch.

She stopped in the doorway and met their angry looks with one of her own.

"I've called your father," she said quietly. "He's on his way here now."

"Big bloody deal," said Gerry, pouting. "He never does anything."

"That's dinkum," returned his twin, Bobby, with a triumphant smile.

"Do you realize how serious this is?" she asked. She sat down at her desk and tried to think how to reason with them. They were so young to be so out of hand. "Listen. There are other students here, who want to learn. It's my job to try to teach them. It simply isn't possible with the two of you disrupting my class all the time. I don't like sending you to the office. I don't like having to tell your parents that you're causing trouble. But I have a duty to all the other parents whose children are here to get an education."

"Education is a lot of rot," Gerry said. "We don't need to go to school. Big Ben never went, and he knows lots of things."

"Big Ben can smell rain," Bobby said. "And track a man through the rain forest."

"Fair go!" Gerry returned. "He knows important things."

She nodded. "Yes, I know. Big Ben used to try to teach me to throw a boomerang. But I never learned."

"I could show you that," Gerry told her. "It's easy."

"He's beaut," Bobby agreed.

She pursed her lips. "Suppose," she said, choosing her words, "that you wanted to show me how to throw a boomerang, Gerry, but two of your classmates kept making noise so you couldn't talk above them. And suppose they hid the boomerang."

Gerry scowled. "Why, I'd knock the bloody stuffings out of them," he said belligerently.

"Perhaps that's how Tim Reilley felt this morning," she continued quietly, "when I was trying to show him how to spell his name, and you and your brother kept scraping your chairs across the floor."

Gerry pondered that. "Well . . ." He looked thoughtful. Perhaps the twins would consider what she'd said.

"I hear your uncle took you out on the muster Saturday," Priss offered, changing the subject.

They brightened immediately at that. "Yes, and he showed us how the ringers cut out bullocks, and how to toss a rope!" Gerry said enthusiastically, all eyes.

"One of the cows got her head caught in the fence," Bobby interrupted, "and Uncle John said some words he told us not to repeat."

She smiled involuntarily, picturing the scene. "Yes, I imagine so."

"Uncle John can do anything," Gerry continued. His face fell. "I wish my dad could ride a horse like that."

"But your dad is grand at figures, did you know?" Priscilla told him. "He can add columns of figures in his head, faster than a calculator. I've seen him. And he's a whiz at math."

"Our dad?" Bobby asked.

"Yes, your dad," she agreed. "He won a scholarship to college because he was so good at it."

"How about that, mate?" Gerry asked his brother.

"But he studied very hard," she continued solemnly. "He sat and paid attention in class and did his homework."

Gerry shifted restlessly in his chair. "They took away the telly," he complained, looking up at her with accusing eyes. "And Mom left again. She said it was because she couldn't stand us around her. And it's all your fault."

Oh, Latrice, how could you? she thought, aching for that small proud boy.

"Your mother was upset, and she didn't mean to hurt you. She loves you. So does your dad. You're very special to them."

"Then, why do they ignore us all the time?" Gerry persisted.

"Your dad's trying to make a living, so he can support you all," she began. "If he didn't work hard, you'd be poor."

"Like Uncle John was?" Bobby broke in, wide-eyed. "Dad said Uncle John didn't have a bean before we came to live with him, but I guess he's got some money now, because he bought me a truck."

Priss stared at the boy with a puzzled frown. She was going to explain that John wasn't poor, but before she could, Randy came into the room, looking angry and impatient and out of sorts.

"You lot are going to ruin me," he accused the boys, growling at them. "I had to pass up an offer on two young bulls I was trying to see, because of you."

"We're sorry," Gerry said, approaching his father with adoring eyes. "We didn't mean to be bad, honest we didn't."

"Dinkum, Dad," Bobby seconded. "We really didn't."

Priscilla stood up. "Why don't you boys walk down the hall a bit? It's ten minutes before we start class."

"Thanks, Miss Priscilla," Gerry said. "We'll

go look at the bird nest outside Mrs. Gaines's window. Come on, mate!"

Bobby ran out behind him, and Priss folded her hands in front of her. "I'm sorry," she apologized. "Something has to be done. They seem penitent right now, but I can't go on letting them disrupt the class. You must see that."

Randy was wearing a business suit but no hat, and he seemed haggard. He sat down in the chair beside her desk and fumbled to light a cigarette.

"I'm at my rope's end," he said. "We restricted the television. We gathered up most of their toys and put them away. We even spanked them. None of it worked. Their mother ran off again to some social affair in Bermuda, and I just haven't time for them."

"Randy," she said, as gently as she could, "that's the whole problem. Nobody has time for them. Children who misbehave as often as not do it to get attention. They don't care whether it's positive attention or not, as long as they get it from someone. But I have a responsibility to the other parents to provide an atmosphere in which their children can learn. I'm not able to do that with the twins disrupting my class. And right now they're furious with me. They seem to blame me for the loss of their television *and* their mother."

He looked oddly guilty. "That's my fault,"

he confessed. "I was muttering about how if you hadn't come to the house . . ."

"Yes, I understand. But the boys are too young to separate angry words from honest ones. They said Latrice told them she couldn't stand them. They took that literally, too."

He smoked quietly, looking defeated. "I love my kids, Priss. But we shouldn't have had them so soon. Latrice was used to being waited on hand and foot until she married me. I had money, of course, but not as much as she was used to. There were so many adjustments. And then having to come up here five years ago, to take over the Run . . ."

She felt herself going pale. Five years? . . . "What?"

"Didn't anyone ever tell you?" he asked. "I realize that John didn't want you to know in the beginning, but now that things are improving, I thought—no matter. He lost it, you see. The whole property. Everything. I had to bail him out or he'd have gone into receivership." He searched her stunned face. "Didn't you know?"

Chapter Eight

If she hadn't been sitting down, her knees would have given way under her. She sat staring at Randy without even seeing him while the words repeated themselves in her numb mind. John had gone bankrupt. He'd gone bankrupt. And she'd never even known. There had been a conspiracy of silence all around: even her parents had kept it from her. But why? Why?

"I'm sorry," Randy said gently. "I didn't realize it would hit you so hard, Priss, or I'd never have said anything."

She straightened. Her heart ran wild in her chest. "Why didn't someone tell me?"

He shrugged. "I thought you knew. It was

all over the district when it happened." He crushed out his cigarette in the ashtray on her desk.

She wasn't sure she could stand up. She felt as sick as she'd ever been in her life. All she could think about was her own cruelty to him since she'd been home, the way she'd ridiculed his clothing . . . and he was such a proud man. Oh, God, what had she done?

Her hands went into the drawer to produce a tissue. She dabbed at her eyes.

"I'm sorry if I upset you," he said.

She looked up. "You pulled the station out of the fire, I gather?"

He started to speak, ran a hand through his hair, and smiled bitterly. "I was a first-class wowser, if you want to know," he told her. "I lorded it over John and crushed what little pride he had left, and walked around with a head like a draft beer. I was going to show big John that I could run rings around him in business." He stared at his clasped hands on his knees. "And at the end of the first year, I'd fouled up everything. I almost lost my own station in New South Wales, and the Sterling Run was no better off. I was desperate enough to ask John for help. He hadn't seemed to care up until then, about anything. But after that, he and I put our heads together and came up with a plan. We're progressing slowly, but we've restocked and reinvested, and we're back on the way to prosperity. I managed to hold on to the sheep station down in New South Wales, and if everything goes well, Latrice and I can move back there in a few months. Maybe she'll settle better near her people."

She stared at the desk. "Yes, perhaps."

He stood up. "Priss, I'll promise you that Latrice and I will make the effort with the twins. I'll try to arrange my schedule so I have more time to give them. Meanwhile, if you have any more problems, let me know. If necessary, I'll cart them off to military school."

She started to protest, but she held her tongue. A teacher could only interfere up to a point. Ultimately it would have to be Randy and Latrice's decision, not hers.

"Thanks for coming, Randy," she said, forcing a smile.

He nodded. "Are you sure you're okay?"

She averted her eyes and mumbled something. He left and the children filed back in from lunch.

Waiting for school to be over was the most difficult thing she'd ever had to do. And as the hours went by, her temper blazed up like a gasoline-soaked fire. By the time the final bell rang, she was out for blood. The first person she went after was her father. She ran him to ground outside in the parking lot and stared at him with wild, hurting eyes.

"Why didn't you tell me about John Sterling?" she asked quietly. "Why did you keep his bankruptcy from me?"

He looked uncomfortable. More than uncomfortable. He ran his hand around the back of his neck with a sigh. "By that time you'd broken up with him," he began, as if he was choosing his words very carefully. "It didn't seem necessary to tell you."

Her eyes stung with unshed tears. "Yes, but I've said some horrible things to him since I've been back. And all because I didn't know the situation. I feel horrible!"

He avoided her gaze. "I'm sorry, darling. Really sorry. But we promised . . ." He cleared his throat. "I mean, we promised each other we wouldn't say anything to you. We didn't realize the problems we might be creating, if that's any excuse."

She stared down at the ground, feeling betrayed and sick and ashamed, all at once. "I have to go and see him," she said.

He studied her bent head. "Yes. That might be the best way," he murmured absently. "Drive carefully. Are you all right?"

"I've just had a shock, that's all," she replied numbly. "I'll be home in a little while."

And with a forced smile, she got into the little secondhand Datsun her father had bought for her, and headed straight for the Sterling Run. She knew Randy would be picking up the twins, and luckily Latrice was away. Priss didn't really want an audience for her interview with John. It would be awkward enough as it was!

Her hands were shaking so, she had trouble keeping the little car on the road as she sped across the cattle grids and past the white fences to the Sterling Run. She was on her way to the front door when she heard voices down at the stables, a short walk away. She turned and headed resolutely down the dirt path.

John was saying something to Big Ben, the aboriginal stockman, who looked past him to spot Priss and grinned toothlessly from ear to ear. He swept off his stockhat and greeted her, his curly white hair gleaming in the sunlight.

"Hello, Missy," he called. "Plurry long time you go away, thought you deadfella. Good you come again."

"Thanks, Ben," she said. "I still haven't learned to throw a boomerang, but at least now I can spell it!"

He grinned and turned away to mount his horse, then rode off to carry out whatever instructions John had given him.

John stared at her, taking in her pale cheeks and pained expression.

"Well, what's your problem?" he growled.

She didn't even reply. She just stared at him and searched for words. Yes, she could see it all now. The khaki trousers and dingo boots, the wide-brimmed Stetson and faded khaki bush shirt half open over his brawny hair-covered chest—they were all old. But she had a feeling the best he owned now wasn't much better than what he had on. The Ford was an economy car. And there had been many bits of conversation about hard times at the Run. All of it came back to haunt her, most of all her own haughty remarks about the suit he'd worn to her homecoming party.

Tears shimmered in her wide eyes, and her lower lip trembled precariously as she looked up. "Randy told me the truth," she said unsteadily and watched his eyes blaze with sudden anger. "Can you imagine how I feel?"

He seemed to turn to stone at the question, at the pity that was plain in her eyes. He let out his breath slowly, and there was a dangerous look on his face as he studied her. "By God, I'll break his back . . . !"

"Why?" she cried brokenly. "Why didn't you tell me? Was that why you broke the engagement—because you went broke? John, for God's sake, I wouldn't have turned my back on you just because you weren't rich! I'd have been back here like a shot, I'd have helped . . . !"

His jaw tightened as he looked down. He turned away to light a cigarette. As he moved the muscles rippled in his powerful arms, and she could hardly bear to be so near him without touching him.

"I had all I could handle," he said after a minute. He stared off down the dirt road that led between the paddocks, where fat Merino sheep were grazing. "Bankruptcy and marriage are a poor combination. And," he added coldly, "there was your age."

She wrapped her arms around herself, staring at his tall form, so alien to her now, so different. "I was growing up fast."

He laughed, without amusement, and turned back. "You wanted me," he said flatly. "And I wanted you. But love wasn't part of it, despite your romantic little daydreams."

"That's not true," she protested, and tears filled her eyes. She went close to him, sympathy mingling with regret in her soft oval face as she stared up at him with the same eyes that had once adored him. "I wouldn't have cared what you had. I'd have stuck by you, no matter what."

"Don't pity me," he ground out. His eyes frightened her. "My bloody oath, I won't have that from you!"

"John," she whispered tearfully. "You did care, a little, didn't you?"

His nostrils flared. He slammed the cigarette down into the dust and made a grab for her. Without another word, he lifted her roughly in his arms and carried her into the deserted barn, shocking her speechless. There was one stall off the neat, clean aisle where hay was kept. He carried her in there and threw her into the golden softness, slinging his hat to one side as he loomed over her.

"Let me show you how much I cared," he said roughly and slid down against her prone body so quickly, she didn't have time to avoid him.

She fought with him, but he only threw a powerful leg across both of hers and held her down. His eyes gleamed with some violent emotion as he searched hers, his hands pinning her wrists to the straw-covered ground.

"I wanted you," he repeated, holding her still. He eased his body completely over hers, letting her feel what was happening to him, watching her face flush and her eyes dilate as the contact made her stiffen. "As you can feel, I still do," he added with a mocking smile. "But that's all it was, all it is, with me. I loved your body, Priss." His eyes devoured the soft form pinned beneath his body, and his heart began pounding, his breath backed up in his throat.

"I loved it . . ." His voice trailed off as he drew his lips suddenly over the erect peak of her breast, which was outlined against the thin fabric of the green dress. His hands released her wrists to slide under her and hold her to him.

She stiffened more and gasped. Her hands caught in his thick blond hair and tried to pry him away, but he only laughed huskily.

"You used to like this," he reminded her tauntingly. "Lie still. No one's going to disturb us here. We can go all the way this time. You're not a shy little virgin anymore."

She opened her mouth to correct that impression and felt his lips cover it. She meant to fight; she wanted to. But it had been five years, and the feel of his hard smoky mouth on hers was intoxicatingly close to heaven. She relaxed very slowly into the hay, feeling the warmth of his lips as they opened, parting hers at the same time. Her hands stopped tugging his hair and eased around to his rough cheeks. She stroked his face, feeling the corners of his mouth with her thumbs, feeling it kissing hers. . . .

He moaned softly, as the tiny caress aroused him, and his hands smoothed over her breasts with tender possession. He bit at her mouth in a familiar remembered way, and she opened her lips to let his tongue probe inside.

His fingers went between them to unbutton his shirt. He took one of her hands from his face and edged it under the fabric, bunching her fingers against one hard male nipple.

"Stroke me there," he whispered gruffly.

Her rebellious fingers liked that telltale sign, and they obeyed him without protest. His mouth grew rougher, more demanding. His hands cupped her breasts and shaped them, his thumbs arousing them even through two layers of fabric. She hated the dress and the bra she wore under it, she wanted her flesh laid bare to his hands, and she gasped in protest when he removed them.

"Priss," he breathed into her mouth. He kissed her harder, with blatant possession. His big rough hands went under her dress and undergarments then, and he slid them along the silken skin of her thighs in a caress more intimate than any they'd ever shared.

She stiffened, catching his hands in her own. Her eyes were wide and a little frightened, her mouth swollen and moist from his kisses.

"No one will see us," he assured. His voice was like velvet, deep and slow. "You want me, don't you?"

"John, you don't . . . understand." She fought to explain before it was too late, before her weakness gave him what he wanted.

"Aren't you on the pill?" he asked. His hands gave in to her renewed protest and moved back up to shelter her head from the hay. "Is that why?"

"No, I'm not on the pill," she rejoined breathlessly. "I never have been. John, I . . . I haven't . . . nothing's changed about my body. I mean . . ."

His glazed eyes began to focus, as sanity came back with a rush. "Are you trying to tell me you're still a virgin?" he asked. "My oath, that's rich!" he added with a cold laugh. He searched for her mouth, but she jerked her face away.

"It's the truth!"

"Of course it is." His hands moved back under the skirt, roughly demanding, and his mouth crushed over hers fiercely. "Stop pretending, Priscilla," he bit off.

"Go ahead, then!" she said angrily, eyes searing him. "Go ahead! You'll find out for yourself, but it will be too late!"

She gritted her teeth and waited. He was strong enough to force her and she knew it. But she hoped his integrity would be enough to save her. And it was.

He let her go and sat up. His big body was shaking with the effort it took, and his eyes were savage, but he breathed deeply and slowly until his heartbeat slackened. His hands smoothed back his disheveled hair, and he stared down at her with an expression that made her blood run cold.

"I feel like a Saturday night special," she managed with a trembling, hard laugh. She avoided his eyes as she sat up and rearranged her clothing. "Like a streetwalker."

He got to his feet and leaned over to sweep up his Stetson and cock it over one eye. He held out a hand with obvious reluctance, but she ignored it and scrambled to her feet alone.

"So now I know," she said, white-faced. She pulled hay out of her hair with trembling fingers. "I know exactly why you proposed. It was the only way you could get me, and you knew it, is that it? Your conscience wouldn't let you seduce your neighbor's teenage daughter!"

He lifted his chin. "Call it a fleeting noble gesture." His eyes narrowed as he watched her body. "I wanted you until it was an obsession."

She swallowed. "So I saw."

His face went hard and cold. "It was only that. I never mentioned loving you."

"That's true," she managed huskily. "You never did." She forced a wan smile and turned away. "We both had a lucky escape, don't you think?"

She averted her eyes and wrapped her arms around her chilled body. All the illusions were gone now. Every one. She realized she'd been living on the thought that he might have cared. On the hope that once she was all grown up he would realize what he had been missing. But now she knew the truth. That it could never be more than desire for him.

Her hands absently smoothed her arms, and John watched her with pained eyes.

She took a steadying breath and let it out.

"Well, what do they say about being cruel to be kind?" she avowed. Her eyes searched his craggy face, the dimple in his chin, the new lines in the deeply tanned flesh. "Thanks. I know exactly where I stand now."

She started back to the car, and he watched her hungrily.

His eyes closed. His fists clenched. "Priss," he whispered, his deep voice anguished.

But she didn't hear him. She climbed into her car and drove away without once looking back.

Chapter Nine

It took Priscilla the rest of the day to get herself back together. She put on a good face in front of her parents, but it took all her willpower not to break down.

"Are you all right, darling?" Renée asked Priss when she came home. "Your father told me what happened. I'm sorry we had any part in hurting you. It's just—"

"It's all right," Priss lied, smiling gamely. "I'm okay now."

Renée hugged her and mumbled something grateful, and later her father accepted Priss's remark that at last she and John understood each other. She went to bed early, and finally was able to let loose the tears that had been building ever since she'd left the Sterling Run that afternoon.

She was convinced now that John felt nothing for her, never had. What a pity, she told herself bitterly, that she'd kept holding on to old memories.

She got up bleary-eyed and managed to go through the motions of teaching. But her appearance gave her away.

"Well, I must say, you look like an accident victim," Ronald George remarked in the corridor as she hurried to class.

She stuck out her tongue at the dark-headed Englishman. "You should see the accident!"

He chuckled, waved, and went on his way.

The twins were well-behaved as they had been the day before, but they looked preoccupied. At the end of the day, Priss asked them why.

"Oh, it's Uncle John," Gerry remarked, and Priss's heart leapt wildly.

"What's wrong with him?" she asked, trying to sound casual.

"We don't know," Bobby said. "He was horrible yesterday. But he hollered real loud when we tried to wake him up this morning, and Daddy said he'd had too many stubbies and was inked."

"Dinkum," Gerry added. "He had a black eye, too."

"In a blue, I'll wager," Bobby remarked enthusiastically. "His knuckles was bleeding, too."

Priss didn't catch the slip of grammar. She was trying to unravel the tangle of Australian slang. Inked was drunk. A blue was a fight. John had been drinking stubbies—beer—and got drunk and had a fight. She blinked. Was that normal behavior, she wondered, or did it have something to do with their confrontation on Monday? Then she realized she was flattering herself. John hadn't batted an eye when she left the Run. As if he cared that he'd hurt her . . . !

"He was as game as Ned Kelly, though, Miss Priscilla," Gerry put in, mentioning a legendary Australian outlaw, "'cause he got up and went out to help with the sheep-shearing regardless of his head."

"I hope he's better," Priss said noncommittally.

"Who, me?" Ronald George grinned, sticking his head in the door.

She laughed. "No."

"Have a coffee with me before you go home," he invited. "I'll make it."

"You can make coffee?" she gasped.

He glowered at her and made a fist. "Know thy place, woman!"

"Watch thy step, man," she returned.

He left, and the twins watched her bright

smile suspiciously. She couldn't know, of course, that they'd make so much out of her laughing repartee with Ronald. But what they did was to go home and tell everyone, including John, that Miss Priscilla was sweet on Mr. George.

"He even made her coffee," Gerry said over his rice pudding.

"Exciting, innit?" Bobby grinned, running the words together in fine Australian fashion. "Bet they'll get married!"

John, who'd been listening to this enthusiastic revelation with a grim, unsmiling face that was bruised and cut, put down his fork, ignored his coffee, and left the table. The twins soon excused themselves as well and ran out to watch the shearing.

"What's wrong with John?" Latrice asked carelessly, wondering at this odd behavior on her first night back from Bermuda. "He barely touched his meal."

Randy grimaced. "I told Priss he went bankrupt five years ago," he sighed. "He all but knocked me about for it, too, I'll tell you. Then he went out and got drunk and beat up a couple of neighboring stockmen." He shook his head as he finished his coffee. "Poor old bloke. He thought she felt sorry for him, you see. Because he's living a deprived life," he added.

"Well, I can understand that," Latrice said

with a venomous smile. "God knows it isn't easy, living in deprivation."

"Steak every night, trips around the world, a new fur every winter, you call that damned deprivation?" he roared.

"Yes, I do!" she shot back. And the subject of John was rapidly replaced by a rundown of problems ending with the twins.

"You've got to take them in hand!" Randy shouted.

"Keep bothering me about those boys, and I'll leave you!" she retorted. She slammed her napkin down and stood up. "I never wanted children in the first place! I won't be hounded about them!"

"They can't be allowed to terrorize the school!"

"Then, ship them off to boarding school, for all I care!"

"Some mother you are," he returned murderously. "Some fine mother!"

She had the grace to look ashamed. And when she turned, the twins were standing there with devastation in their young faces.

"I told you, didn't I?" Gerry asked his brother with trembling lips. "I told you she hated us!"

"You . . . you old cow!" Bobby shouted.

They both ran out the door at the same time, leaving their parents standing horrified in the hallway.

"Gerry, Bobby, come back, I didn't mean it!" Latrice called. She ran to the door, but they were already out of sight. She turned a white face to Randy. "What shall we do?"

Randy turned. "I'll go get John."

Priss had walked down to the creek behind her father's property and was sitting quietly under a big gum tree. She was wearing jeans and a pink T-shirt and sneakers and trying not to remember what had happened the day before.

She hadn't been able to sit still in the house. The memory of John's rough ardor was too fresh. She was toying with the idea of going back to Hawaii, of escaping even the threat of his company, when she heard a crashing noise on the other bank.

She looked up, and there were the terrible twins, rushing headlong toward the wide stream. They didn't even seem to notice her. It was obvious they'd been crying profusely.

"Gerry, Bobby! What's wrong?" she called, getting to her feet.

"We're running away from home," Gerry called back.

They kept coming, right through the stream, hardly pausing to avoid the slick rocks.

"Where will you go?" Priss asked reasonably.

"We'll go to Brisbane and get jobs delivering papers," Gerry said matter-of-factly. "And we'll get a hotel room."

"With what?"

Gerry reached in his pocket, his tearstained face very proud and mature. "I have five dollars. See?"

She could have cried. They looked so miserable, and she remembered from her own childhood how helpless it felt to be totally dependent on adults, with no rights at all.

She went down on one knee and stared Gerry in the eyes. "Tell me what happened."

"Mom doesn't want us," he whispered brokenly and collapsed in tears.

"Oh, Gerry," she said gently. She gathered the two of them into her arms and just held them while they cried, and they didn't even make an effort to pull away. Just a little love, she thought silently. That was all they needed —just a little love and consistent discipline.

A sound brought Priss's head up. John was standing on the opposite bank.

He was bareheaded for once, his blond-streaked hair shimmering in the dappled sunlight, and his face looked worn and haggard. One eye was black and blue, and there was a cut on his chin.

"We're up a gum tree," Gerry moaned as he watched his uncle come across the stream with slow steady strides.

"He's narked, too," Bobby said resignedly.

But apparently he wasn't angry at the boys. He didn't fuss or accuse. He simply bent down, as Priss had done, and opened his arms. They ran to him.

"Your mother's sorry," he said without preamble. "She and your dad had a fight. You caught the tail end. You know, sometimes adults say things without meaning them."

"If she doesn't mean them," Gerry began, "why does she keep saying them, Uncle John?"

John sighed angrily and looked up, meeting Priss's quiet eyes. She averted hers, because she couldn't bear the sight of him. Was he thinking of the terrible things they had said to each other in the heat of anger?

"Your mom and dad are having some problems," John said finally. "They'll work them out. But until they do, you have to try not to take everything they say to heart."

"They won't bust up, will they?" Bobby interrupted, wiping his tears on a grubby sleeve. "Gee, that would be horrible!"

"They won't bust up," John said grimly. "Now let's go back. Your parents are frantic."

"Okay," Gerry mumbled reluctantly. He looked over his shoulder at Priss. "See you tomorrow, Miss Priscilla."

"Me, too," Bobby seconded. He started across the stream after his brother.

"Wait for me at the Land-Rover," John called to them, his deep voice carrying easily.

Priss started to leave, but he got between her and the path.

"I'm sorry," he said. "I didn't mean to hurt you like that. I said some things I didn't mean. Dammit, Priss, I couldn't bear your pity."

She avoided his eyes and backed away from him, a movement that brought his dark brows together.

"As you said yourself at the outset," she murmured, trying to sound calm, "it's all behind us now. Will you move out of my way, please?"

He searched for the right words, and couldn't find them. He ran his fingers through his thick sunbleached hair. "We could . . . start again," he suggested.

She stared at his dusty boots. "I don't want to. Not anymore," she added, and looked straight up into his eyes. "That makes twice you've pushed me away. I won't bother you again. Not ever. And when I finish out this school year, John, I'm going back to Hawaii."

His face went pale under his tan. "Hawaii?" he faltered.

She hadn't really decided that, but she liked the impact it made on him. Good, let him be upset! Why should she suffer alone?

"I loved Hawaii," she said. "I miss it."

His eyes searched hers for a long time. "We had a lot going for us," he tried again.

"What? Desire?" She laughed bitterly and saw him flinch.

"Why are you still a virgin?" he demanded, taking the direct approach. "If you really stopped caring about me, why hasn't there been a man?"

She held on to her nerve, but it took all the willpower she had. "I'm not that kind of girl, remember?" she asked and turned away.

"Five years is a long time," he said. "We could get acquainted again."

"Why bother?" she asked carelessly. "You've made it more than obvious that all you need is a body. Mine," she added venomously, "is not on the market."

"Priss," he growled.

"So why don't you get lost?" she told him. "Go get in another blue or barney or whatever else you call it, but leave me alone, John Sterling. I'm off men for life!"

She edged around him, deliberately avoiding any contact with his hard body, and stormed off toward the house.

He frowned after her. After a moment, with a grimly determined smile, he turned and strode off toward the creek and the Land-Rover beyond.

The twins announced the next day that their parents had gone off somewhere to straighten themselves out. They were quieter, but she noticed a new confidence in their eyes as they went through the school days. Perhaps they knew now that they were loved, she thought. It made all the difference to children.

She wouldn't think about the difference it would make to her. She hadn't one single shred of hope left about John Sterling. If only there were some eligible man she could start dating to show John how little she cared! She even considered Ronald George. But he was hopelessly smitten with Amanda now, and it wouldn't be fair to use him, anyway.

At the end of the day, she was gathering her things up before leaving when John walked into the classroom. Her eyes widened as he paused silently in the doorway, big and rugged-looking in his tan bush shirt and khaki pants and dingo boots. He had his hat in one hand, and the other worried his blond-streaked hair.

"Yes?" she asked icily.

One corner of his mouth curled. "Declaring war?" he mused.

"You did that for me," she returned, green eyes flashing.

His dimpled chin lifted, and he smiled softly. "In the hay, you mean?" he questioned.

She flushed and almost dropped the study guide in her hand. She recovered it just in time with a fumble.

"Did you want something in particular? I would like to go home," she said formally.

"The boys and I are going on a picnic Saturday," he said. "We'd like you to come with us."

The invitation caught her off guard. "Why me?" she hedged.

He shrugged. "They like you."

"And you'll suffer my company on their behalf, is that it?" she threw back. "I'm busy Saturday, thanks."

"Why won't you come, Priscilla?" he taunted. "Are you afraid you might not be able to keep your hands off me?"

She aimed the book at his head, but he held up a hand.

"If you throw it," he challenged, "I'll find a newer, more interesting use for that desk behind you."

His eyes told her what he meant, and she bit her lower lip, half afraid to find out if he was kidding or not. She tucked the book back in the crook of her arm.

"What a pity," he wondered. "I was looking forward to that."

"Save your line for some other woman, John Sterling. I'm immune," she shot back.

"Good. I won't have to shake you off," he said carelessly. "Come with us. The fresh air would do you good, and the twins could use a little womanly companionship."

"No." She forced herself to say it without flinching or feeling regret. Why was he doing this to her?

His blue eyes searched her green ones for a long quiet moment. "I've apologized."

"It doesn't change anything," she continued. "You want me. But I've already told you graphically that I'm not available in that way."

"Yes, I know," he said, watching her with a faint smile. "Fascinating, isn't it, how you've kept yourself chaste all these years. And there I was, thinking you just felt sorry for me. . . ."

"Well, hello," Ronald George interrupted, stopping by to lean over John's shoulder. "Nice to see you, Mr. Sterling. How about some coffee, Priscilla?"

"Thank you, that would be lovely, Ronald," she said, with a sweet smile. "I'll be there in a minute."

"I'll put it on, love. Good day, Mr. Sterling."

Ronald went off down the hall, and John's face grew stormy. His eyes glittered down at Priss.

"What do you see in that pommy?" he demanded.

"Refinement," she shot right back. "He'd never think of dragging me into a hay stall!"

"Thank God," he exhaled, putting his hat back on.

"That's exactly what I say!" she replied. "He's a gentleman!"

"You never used to fight with me," he mused. "I like you this way, Priss. You've grown into a passionate woman."

He was making her uncomfortable. She shifted her weight to the other foot. "Look, John, we can't go back . . ."

"I don't want to," he told her. "I want to go ahead. I want to get to know you all over again."

"Stop confusing me," she ground out. "I don't want this, I don't want to get involved with you . . . !"

"Are you coming, Priscilla?" Ronald George called from down the hallway.

"Buckley's chance, mate!" John called back in his deep drawl.

"Don't mind him!" Priss interrupted angrily.

"Who's Buckley?" Ronald asked. "And what chance?"

"My bloody oath, where did the education department dig him up?" John growled. He glared at Priss. "Are you coming Saturday?"

"I told you. No."

He sighed angrily. "You're enough to make a man go walkabout."

"I thought you'd already done that," she said with a cold smile. "Your eye's much better. Only yellowish, now, isn't it?" she added.

He averted his face. "A man's entitled to an occasional difference of opinion."

"You didn't used to fight," she said.

"I didn't used to do a lot of bloody things," he grated. He studied her soft face irritatedly. "Nothing like a woman to drive a man to drink!"

"My, we are in a bad temper, aren't we?" she provoked.

He glared down at her through narrowed eyes. "Why won't you come picnicking?"

"Because I hate you!" she threw back.

"Oh, Priscilla . . . !" Ronald George called gaily.

"You're getting on my quince, parcel post!" John shouted down the hall.

"I say, old man, I never touched your quince! And what's that about a package . . . ?" Ronald called back.

John took a deep breath. "You're annoying me, newcomer," he translated.

"One might have said so, mightn't one?" Ronald reacted as he started back up the hall.

"Oh, bloody hell!" John growled. He gave Priss one last glare and stomped off down the corridor.

"Good day, Mr. Ster . . . oof!"

There was a hard thud, and Priss ran out into the hall to find Ronald George sitting in the middle of the floor looking stunned.

"Whatever happened?" she gasped. She helped him up and watched him dust himself off.

"Big fellow, isn't he?" Ronald noted with a groggy smile. "I didn't get out of the way fast enough apparently. How about that coffee?"

She escorted him into the teachers' lounge with a thoughtful stare toward the exit, where John had disappeared.

If she'd expected John to give up about the picnic, she had a surprise in store. He drove up unexpectedly after supper Friday night at her parents' home.

"John," Adam greeted him, "come in and join us. We were just watching the international news."

"Would you like some coffee, John?" Renée offered, smiling as she put aside her crocheting and got to her feet.

Priss sat nervously curled up in her big armchair, dressed in faded too-tight jeans and a shrunken red T-shirt with no bra underneath. Her feet were bare, and John glanced at her with a slow smile. She could have thrown the television at him.

"I'd love a cup, thanks, Renée. How are things, Adam?"

Her father motioned John to the armchair next to Priss's and sat down himself across the room.

"Going very well. I, uh, hear you and Ronald George had a confrontation a couple days ago," Adam remarked with a grin.

John looked irritated. "Damned fool walked out in front of me. I had things on my mind," he added, glancing toward Priss.

"Nice man, George," Adam murmured with a wry glance at Priss. "Excellent teacher. We're lucky to get him." He put down his coffee cup. "How about a game of chess?"

"Haven't time tonight; worst luck," John

told him. "I came to ask Priscilla to go picnicking with the twins and me tomorrow."

Priss bit her lower lip. So that was his game. He couldn't get her to go on his own, so he was going to enlist her parents' aid!

"I told you—" she began.

"Good," Adam said firmly. "She could use some free time; she's worked like a Trojan ever since she's been back."

"But—" she continued.

"How true," Renée concurred, smiling when John took the silver tray from her and put it on the coffee table. "Here's yours, John," she said, serving him. "Priss, I brought one for you, too."

"Thanks, Mom," Priss said. "There's just—" she tried again.

"My thoughts exactly," John butted in. He crossed his long legs and grinned at Priss. "The change of scenery will do you good."

"I had planned—" she began once more.

"And she had nothing to do tomorrow, anyway," Renée added quickly. "We'll put together a picnic basket here, so you won't have to go to the trouble, John."

"Just so," Adam added, beaming at her. "She'll enjoy it."

Priss sighed wearily and gave up. But her eyes told John Sterling exactly what she thought of him.

"Darling, this might be a good time to go

over the budget, since Priss is here to talk to John. You don't mind, John, do you?" Renée added, grinning. "We'll only be thirty minutes or so. Come on, Adam," she prodded to her husband, dragging him out of his chair by the arm. "We'll just sit in the kitchen and work on it."

Priss's father was trying to say something, but he was unceremoniously bundled out of the room before he could get it out.

John caught her eyes and held them as he sipped his coffee. "Go ahead. Let it out. You look mad as hell."

"Oh, no," she grumbled. "Everything's apples!"

He smiled slowly. "You sound like a native already."

"And don't butter me up," she added. "I don't want to go on your damned picnic!"

"The boys will be disappointed. I told them you would."

"Why? You might have asked me first!"

"Listen." He set down his cup and leaned forward, his hairy forearms crossed over his knees. "All I want is conversation. Just to talk. The twins would make anything else between us impossible, so what are you afraid of?"

"I won't get involved with you," she said firmly. "Not physically or otherwise."

He cocked an eyebrow. "Did I ask you to?"

"What do you want from me?"

"I'm lonely," he said simply. "I could use someone to talk to. A friend, if you like."

"You want us to be friends?" she asked incredulously. "After what's happened . . . ?"

"I don't want us to be enemies," he replied, and his voice was like black velvet. "Do you?"

She stared down at her curled-up legs. "No, I guess not."

"Then, suppose we try getting along for short stretches?"

She looked up with all her unvoiced fears in her eyes.

"I won't touch you, Priscilla," he assured her gently. "You've nothing to fear from me physically. I won't even try to hold hands."

"That's comforting," she reflected, dropping her eyes.

"I thought you might feel that way. As I said, the boys will protect you from me." He lifted his cup again and sat back. "If you really want to be protected," he added with a maddening smile.

She felt her face going hot and kept it down so he wouldn't see the wild color in her cheeks. "I got carried away before."

"So did I, love," he confided quietly, and his deeply tanned face was suddenly grave. "We were good together, that way, from the very first time we kissed."

"Dragging up the past won't help things," she declared stubbornly.

"I do realize that," he agreed. He sipped his coffee. "I've spent five years trying to put it all out of my mind. I haven't been quite successful." His eyes caught hers. "And I don't think you have, either."

"I'm working on it," she echoed with a cool smile.

"With that pommy?" he grumbled.

"Ronald George is a nice man," she tossed back.

His nostrils flared as he tried to control his temper. He set the coffee cup down carefully and got to his feet. "I'd better go before I lose my temper again."

"Perhaps you'd better," she countered sweetly.

He glowered at her. "The boys and I will pick you up about eight."

"I'll be ready." She got up as well, finding herself all too close to him. She could feel the warmth of his large body; smell the clean scent of it mingled with his spicy cologne.

"Even in old clothes you're quite something, Priscilla Johnson," he said softly.

She looked up and noticed that he was blatantly staring at her. She crossed her arms over her breasts.

"Stop that," she grumbled.

"Does it bother you, remembering?" he quietly mocked.

The color in her cheeks blazed. She turned

away toward the hall and quickly opened the front door for him.

"I'm being evicted, I see," he lamented. He paused in the doorway, grinning wickedly. "Tell your parents I said good night." His eyes dropped down again, and he chuckled softly at her irritated movement.

"That's all over," she reminded him coldly.

He studied her flushed face. "I've built my station back up from bankruptcy," he began quietly. "I've literally made something from nothing. I don't have a lot of money. Not yet. But I have one hell of a lot of drive. What I want, I get. So watch out, little sheila."

She swallowed down a lump in her throat. "Don't try to make me into that kind of woman, John," she warned unsteadily.

He frowned slightly. "What the hell are you talking about?"

"There are plenty of women who give out—"

"I don't want you that way," he declared.

"Then . . . what?" she faltered.

He touched her cheek with the tips of his lean fingers, brushing it softly. "Be my friend, Priscilla."

It was all she could do not to catch that large hand and press her mouth against it. But she had to be strong: he was a past master at this game, and she wasn't adept enough.

"Friendship is all I can give you now," she responded.

His eyes dropped to her mouth, then went

back up to meet her gaze. "Good night, love."
He turned and walked away without another
word.

Why did he have to use that endearment,
she wailed silently, and bring back all the
bittersweet memories along with it?

"Has John gone already?" Adam asked as
he and Renée reentered the living room minutes later.

"He had things to do," Priss explained. She
looked from one of her speculating parents to
the other. "It's only going to be friendship,"
she attested firmly. "I can't take any more
rejection from him."

"Of course, dear," Renée said gently. She
bent and kissed her daughter on the forehead.
"How about some more coffee?"

"I'd love a cup. I'll help you," Priss volunteered.

Renée scrutinized Adam, who winked. She
was glowing as she followed her daughter into
the kitchen.

Chapter Ten

They spread the picnic cloth under a coolabah tree beside a water hole in the stream. Or, as John put it, a billabong.

"Do you know the original words to 'Waltzing Matilda'?" he queried her with a grin. "'Once a jolly swagman camped by a billabong, under the shade of a coolabah tree . . .'"

"I'd forgotten!" she exclaimed.

"The words were written by one of our best poets—Banjo Paterson," he continued, helping her unpack the wicker hamper.

"I have one of his books," Priss volunteered. "He was very good. I liked the poem about Clancy, too . . ."

"'Clancy of the Overflow,'" Gerry chuckled, nudging his brother. "Remember, Dad read it to us once."

"Didn't Clancy turn up in 'The Man from Snowy River', too?" Priss asked John. "I saw the movie and loved it!"

"So did I. Yes, that was Clancy." He searched her eyes slowly. "Australia gets into your blood, doesn't it?"

"It's a big spectacular country," she agreed, dropping her eyes to his blue patterned shirt. "Much like America—especially in its history, its pioneer days."

"Yes, I suppose so. We had our desperadoes, too, like Ned Kelly."

"Can me and Gerry go swimming?" Bobby asked John.

"Sure, take your clothes off and help yourselves, if you aren't ready for your food yet," John told them.

"Bonzer!" Gerry grinned.

The boys stripped down to their swimming trunks and dived into the water.

"Is it safe here?" Priss asked.

"For whom, the boys or you?" he murmured dryly.

She moved restlessly, tugging up the shoulder of the pale blue peasant dress she was wearing. "The boys, of course."

"I didn't expect you to wear a dress," he stated. He was stretched out across from her in the grass, and her eyes helplessly followed the long powerful lines of his body from legs to narrow hips to broad chest straining against his partially unbuttoned shirt. She could see the darker blond hair on his chest, and she tingled with unwanted memories.

"My jeans were all in the wash," she muttered. That was true enough. Her mother had smiled gaily when she'd told Priss there weren't any clean jeans. "Thanks to my mom," she added darkly.

"Her middle name must be Cupid," he said dryly.

"She doesn't know you like I do," she returned icily.

"That's true enough." He toyed with the handle of the wicker hamper. "There aren't many women who do know me the way you do," he added, lifting his eyes to catch hers.

"Only a few hundred, I'm sure," she snapped.

He shook his head. "Only a handful, if you're interested," he said seriously. "I never had time for full-fledged affairs. The station always came first."

"Can't we talk about something else?" she asked miserably. The thought of him with other women, particularly Janie Weeks, was unbearable. Once again she wondered why he had never married the other woman.

"Why are you still a virgin?"

The question knocked her sideways. She stared at him with a mind gone blessedly blank.

"Yes, I know I keep harping on it. But it disturbs me. Did I damage you emotionally, is that it?" he persisted with narrowed, intent eyes. "Or couldn't you feel it with anyone else?"

"You said we were going to be friends!" she burst out.

He shrugged irritably. "Yes, my oath, I did. But I'd still like to know why."

"It's past history. As for my lack of experience," she added, "I never liked the idea of being promiscuous. Since most modern men have an opposite attitude, and word gets around, I didn't date very often. Does that answer your question?"

"I can see it all," he nodded, and smiled gently. "Miss Iceberg. Only you were never that with me. You were warm and soft and giving, and you aroused me as no other woman ever had."

"Only because I was innocent," she said, looking away. "Would you like some fried chicken and potato salad?"

"Because you were you," he corrected. "I'm sorry for what I did to you in the stable. Sorry that I made something distasteful out of it. I had this wild idea that you'd been around," he added slowly. "But once I started, when I realized that you still wanted me—"

"I don't—!" she began.

He reached out and caught her hand. Holding her eyes, he drew her fingers down over her own breast where the hard tip was visible against the soft fabric of her dress.

"You don't what?" he demanded quietly.

She jerked her hand from under his, horrified when, instead of falling away, his fingers landed gently on her breast. She pulled away from him, her eyes wide and accusing.

"As you yourself said," she shot at him, "it's a purely physical reaction. A residue from a dead relationship. Friendship is all I have left to give you."

He dropped his hand to the tablecloth and sifted through the box of plastic forks. "You don't want something a little more physical than that?"

"I don't want an affair," she stated calmly.

He smiled faintly. "Neither do I, oddly enough." He looked up. "Especially not with a virgin."

"Stop making me sound like a dinosaur."

"You're a lovely dinosaur," he remarked, running his eyes over her flushed face framed by its halo of softly curling blonde hair. "Does he turn you on?"

She blinked at the lightning change of subject. "He?"

"That pommy."

"You mean Ronald?" She smiled slowly. "He's very nice."

His face grew cold. "He's young."

"So am I," she reminded him.

He rolled over onto his back, with his arms under his head, and stared up at the sky. "Ten years my junior," he murmured. "It was a hell of a difference five years ago. Almost different generations, Priss."

"Yes."

He turned his head sideways and studied her bent head. "I kept up with you." He surprised her. "Through your parents."

"They knew?" she accused.

"I had to have their cooperation," he said. "I couldn't risk having them tell you the truth, so I swore them to silence." He nodded as her eyes mirrored her surprise.

"You knew me very well, didn't you?" she mocked bitterly.

"Well enough." He observed her. "Someday I'll tell you all of it. But in the meantime try to remember that I spared you some bitter times and some hard memories, will you?"

"And an empty marriage," she added.

He frowned. "What?"

"You said it was all desire on your part, didn't you?" she shot at him coolly. "We'd have been in divorce court as soon as the newness wore off."

He sat up. "Maybe it's time we talked about that—"

"Hey, Uncle John, there's a wombat over here! Can we have it?" Gerry called suddenly.

"No!" he shot back. And, knowing the twins, he got quickly to his feet. "I'd better have a look," he told Priss. "They'll be using it for a volleyball next."

She watched him walk away. He was the

most masculine-looking man she'd ever seen. Muscular and graceful and sensuous. His fair hair caught the sun and gleamed like silver, and when he grinned at the boys, his face became young again, the face she'd loved as a teenager.

She still did love it, if the truth were known. But she couldn't be drawn into an affair with John. It would kill her.

Once the wombat was herded off and the boys had dried themselves, the four of them sat down to their picnic feast. Afterward the boys went back to swim some more, and Priss and John stretched out full-length on the picnic cloth and closed their eyes.

She was aware of him close at her side, and had to steel herself not to flinch every time he moved. She remembered so well another time when they'd lain like this, on Margaret's sofa, and he'd come close to making love to her.

He chuckled softly, and she turned her head sideways to study his relaxed features.

"What was that all about?" she asked.

"I was remembering that night at Margaret's," he reminisced, turning his head to catch her eyes. "You had me so out of my head that I was ready to take you, right there, door unlocked and all."

She flushed, dropping her eyes to his partially unbuttoned shirt. That made her turn even redder, and he laughed more deeply.

"Does it bother you, little prude?" he whispered. "Look."

And he deliberately unbuttoned the rest of the shirt and pulled it free of his slacks, letting her see the rippling muscles of his stomach and chest with their feathering of dark hair.

"John . . ." she protested.

"I like the way you look at me," he avowed huskily, and he wasn't smiling anymore. "I like the feel of your eyes. I like knowing that you want to touch me." He reached out and brushed his fingers over hers, turning her hand so that he was lightly stroking the palm. "You'd like that, wouldn't you?" he asked. "You'd like to come over here and stroke my body the way I used to stroke yours, to watch me shudder and groan with desire."

Her lips parted. He was doing it again, and she was going under like a drowning swimmer.

"Know what I'd do to you, young Priss, if the boys weren't here?" he asked under his breath. "I'd roll you over on your back," he whispered tenderly. "And I'd pull that elastic bodice down to your waist. And then I'd put my mouth—"

"It's getting late," she burst out in a high-pitched little voice as she sat up quickly and then got to her feet.

John got to his own feet and watched her

like a mouse-hungry cat, all mischievous eyes and mocking smiles.

"Nothing's changed," he maintained. "Only the year."

"I've changed," she argued, eyes flashing. "I'm not a naive little teenager anymore!"

"No," he concurred. "You're all woman, and I want you now more than ever."

"You won't get me!" she promised.

"You said we could be friends, didn't you?" he mused.

"Not if you keep saying horrible things to me!"

He grinned, showing his even white teeth. "What did I say that was horrible?"

"About pulling my dress . . ." She swallowed. "You know what."

"That wasn't horrible. It was exciting," he contradicted with a lazy smile. "And that's exactly what I'd have done if the twins hadn't been around. And you'd have let me, Priscilla. You'd have helped me."

"I won't see you again, John," she asserted firmly. She bent to gather up the picnic things, without looking at him.

"Of course you will," he drawled lazily. He tucked his shirt back into his trousers and fastened it halfway up. "Tonight, in fact."

She straightened up and looked at him. "What?"

"Renée invited me to supper."

She'd strangle her mother, she told herself. "I'll go see a movie," she griped.

"You might as well give in," John advised. "You won't win."

She glowered at him. "Yes, I will. I've got too much sense to let myself in for any more heartache!"

He shook his head. "There won't be any heartache this time, little sheila," he softly supplied, and he smiled. "I promise."

"Because you won't get close enough to cause any," she returned.

"We'll see." He lifted his head and called the boys. They came running up, dripping wet, clothes clutched helter-skelter in their hands.

"That was bonzer," Gerry laughed. "Thanks for coming with us, Miss Priscilla, today was just like being a family!"

"Dead right," Bobby agreed.

Priss looked from one to the other. She hadn't realized just how much such an outing might mean to young boys who'd lacked parental affection. She smiled softly at them.

"You could come see us at home, too, Miss Priss," Gerry ventured.

"As a matter of fact, it's lambing and calving over at the Run," John added, watching her. "We've got a mob of babies you could look at."

"Too right!" Gerry agreed. "They're fun to pet, Miss Priscilla."

"Priss used to come over and watch us muster cattle," John volunteered, and his eyes were keen on her face. "Remember, Priss?"

She did, vividly. She'd always been around in spring. John never had seemed to mind, though. He'd take time to show her the newest additions to his herd and watch her enthusiastic response to them.

"You were very patient," she recalled with downcast eyes.

"I still am," he replied. "In every way that counts."

She turned away before he could see the wild rosiness in her cheeks.

"How about it?" he persisted as he helped the twins into the Land-Rover. "Want to come over tomorrow?"

She had to force herself not to give in to the lazy seduction in his voice.

"Not tomorrow," she answered.

He tilted his hat over one eye and smiled. "All right."

That threw her. She'd expected an argument. She faltered a minute before she got into the vehicle and let him close the door.

She was still puzzled that evening as she got ready for dinner. She stood staring at herself in the mirror, wondering why she was bothering to dress up. She wore a gauzy white skirt and pullover blouse, and looked like something out of the twenties—very frilly and feminine.

"It's more than he deserves," she told her reflection.

"Yes, I know, but he is a dish, my darling," Renée said from the door. She grinned like a young girl. "My, he is in hot pursuit these days, isn't he?"

"It won't do him any good," Priss assured her. "I won't be taken in again."

Renée leaned against the doorjamb and watched her daughter brush her short hair. "He's a proud man," she remarked.

"Yes, I know."

"It's not easy for a man like him to admit to weaknesses," she continued. "John was brought to his knees. He didn't want anyone to see him that way. Especially not you."

"He said it was only physical," Priss said quietly. "That he only wanted me."

"With a man, love often comes after physical infatuation," Renée told her.

"Mom," Priss began hesitantly, "whatever happened to Janie Weeks?"

Renée looked uncomfortable for a moment. "She married a fellow in Brisbane . . . shortly after you and John broke up."

Priss turned with scalding eyes to face her mother. "I'm afraid," she confessed. "I just don't want to risk being hurt again. I don't think I could bear it if I got involved with John and then he gave in to physical infatuation for another woman, the way he did with Janie."

"My darling," Renée advised gently, "you mustn't judge John too harshly. He's paid a terrible price for the decisions he made . . . whether they were right or wrong."

John was wearing a blue blazer, white shirt, and white trousers when he arrived for dinner. His blond head was bare, and he looked as urbane as any Brisbane businessman.

"You look nice," Priss complimented reluctantly.

He smiled at her. "So do you. Very roaring twentyish."

"I'm an old-fashioned girl," she reminded him.

"I know," he remarked with a devilish smile, and she dropped her eyes.

"Come on in to the living room while the women get the food on the table," Adam said, "and I'll pour you a brandy."

"That sounds fine," John said. "What do you think about this new political crisis in the States?"

They went off into a long discussion about politics in general while Priss and Renée set the bowls of steaming hot beef and rice and Brussels sprouts and biscuits on the table.

"What's your opinion, Priss?" John asked as they were seated.

"About what?" she asked, going blank as she looked at his rugged face with its dimpled chin and twinkling eyes.

"Oh, I don't know," he murmured, as if staring back at her had knocked a few words out of his head, too. He searched her soft green eyes for a long moment and watched her pupils widen, her lips part. It took all his willpower not to get up and go across the table after her.

She cleared her throat and reached for her glass of iced tea. Not until she'd taken a calming sip of it did she try to talk again, and she didn't look straight into his eyes this time.

"How are things going, John?" Renée asked as they waded through international politics and marked their way back to everyday topics. "This is your busiest time, I recall."

"Yes," he confirmed. "Lambing, calving, mustering, shearing. . . . It's great to get away from the station and all the complaints."

"You've hired on some new men, I hear," Adam remarked.

"Have to." John grinned. "Our own would quit if they had all that work to do alone. Besides, the shearers are a breed apart. It's an experience to watch them in the sheds."

"Indeed it is," Priss agreed. She smiled at him over her coffee cup. "I got to help once."

He cocked an eyebrow. "Yes, you did. I had the only sheep in the river basin with mohawks."

She flushed. "Well, I tried."

"You wouldn't have gotten near my Merinos

if that shearer hadn't been sweet on you," he added, cupping his coffee cup in his big hands. "I watched you, too, just to make sure he didn't get fresh. You were a dish even at sixteen, little Priss."

"Big brother to the rescue," she chided, embarrassed because she'd never told her parents about that.

"Thank God you were around to look out for her," Adam gratefully acknowledged. "She's always been a handful."

"A lovely handful, my darling," Renée said with a smile. "The greatest joy of our lives."

"I was almost the undoing of John a few times," Priss admitted. She glanced at him, and for once all the animosity and bitterness fell away. "I worried you terribly, didn't I?"

"I could have stopped you any time I liked," he confessed. He searched her puzzled eyes. "Or didn't that ever occur to you?"

It hadn't. She studied his craggy face curiously. "Why didn't you?" she asked, her voice soft.

His thumb caressed the porcelain cup absently as he looked back at her. "I liked having you around," he offered quietly. "Despite the fact that we all knew you were years too young to be daydreaming over me," he added with a wicked grin.

"We trusted you," Adam chuckled.

"Of course," Priss submitted. "I was like his kid sister."

John's eyes narrowed, and when she looked into them, she read graphically that in no way had she been like his kid sister.

"How about some dessert?" she asked quickly, and rose to get it.

In the kitchen, she uncovered the Southern pecan pie she'd made and began to slice it. Her heart was wildly racing, and she hoped she could calm down before she went back into the living room.

She felt him before she heard his voice, sensed his presence as if she'd been born with radar.

"Can I help?" John asked at her back.

"I'm just finishing up," she replied. Was that squeaky voice really hers? The kitchen shrank when he walked in.

"I love that pie," he said. "A southern-American specialty, isn't it?"

"Yes," she returned breathlessly. She reached for saucers, but his big hands slid around her waist and she froze, helpless, as his fingers moved, fondling her.

His breath sighed out against the top of her head, and she could feel the warmth of his big body, feel the muscles of his chest against her back. She was drowning again. She wanted to turn and let him crush her body into his; she wanted to lift her face and let him kiss her hungry mouth until she stopped aching.

"Did you bake it?" he asked quietly.

"Yes . . . I . . . I can cook, you know," she faltered.

His chest rose and fell roughly. His hands moved slowly up and down her waist. "You did the lunch today, too, didn't you?" he murmured. "The chicken and potato salad . . ."

She swallowed. "Yes."

He moved an inch closer, bringing his body into total contact with hers, and she caught her breath and stiffened.

"You still smell of gardenias," he whispered in her ear. His mouth touched it and then ran slowly down the side of her neck to her shoulder. "You even taste of them."

The feel of his hard warm mouth was doing crazy things to her willpower. Her head involuntarily went to one side to give him better access to her silky skin.

She felt the edge of his teeth then, and heard the ragged sigh of his breath.

"It's no good," he said roughly. "Turn around and give me your mouth."

She wanted that, too. She needed to taste him, to let him satisfy the aching hungers he'd created. Without a protest, she started to turn, but the sound of footsteps broke them quickly apart.

"Sorry, but there's a phone call for you, John," Adam interrupted, peeking through the door. "Your jackeroo."

"Damn," John muttered darkly. He glanced

ruefully at Priss before he went out the door, and Adam made a regretful face before he followed suit. Priss went back to dishing up the pie, with hands that shook and a body that hurt with unsatisfied need.

By the time she had the dishes on a tray and had carried them into the dining room, John was standing in the hall with Adam.

". . . Damned sorry," John was saying irritably. He glanced toward the dining room. "I have to go," he told her. "A blue down at the shearer's quarters. My jackeroo can't calm them down."

She could imagine John doing that, quite easily. She'd seen him break up fights before.

"We're glad you could come to supper," she told him in a low voice.

His eyes searched hers across the room. "Walk me out."

She went to him without a protest, a sheep going to the slaughter. She barely saw the knowing look her parents exchanged as she took the large hand John held out to her and went with him onto the darkened porch.

"Oh, God, come here, love," he groaned urgently, drawing her trembling body completely against his. "Kiss me . . . !"

His mouth opened as it touched hers, and she met the kiss hungrily, reaching up to hold him, to plaster her aching body to the hardness of his. She clung to the strong muscles of his back, feeling his teeth against her own with the ardent pressure of his devouring mouth.

She moaned helplessly, in the throes of something so explosive it rocked her on her feet, and his arms tightened.

"I need you," he whispered into her mouth. "I need you . . ."

He was trembling, and so was she, and the darkness spun around her like a Ferris wheel while she tried to get enough of his warm demanding mouth, the deep penetration of his tongue, the rough massage of his hands down her spine.

She felt him maneuver their bodies so the porch wall was behind her. Still holding her mouth in bondage, he eased himself down against her, crushing her hips and breasts and thighs under his so she could feel the very texture of his muscles.

She cried out, softly, helplessly, and he lifted his blond head and stared into her eyes in the dim light.

"I want you under me like this in a bed," he said unsteadily, his eyes glittering.

Her nails bit into his back as she tried to find a protest.

"Don't start making excuses," he commanded gruffly. "You want me, too."

"You're heavy," she moaned.

"Yes, and you love it," he breathed against her lips. He moved his hips deliberately and felt her stiffen and clutch at him. "Oh, Priss, I'd give anything to have you alone with me in a dark room for just an hour. Just one hour . . . !"

"I can't," she whispered tearfully. "I can't, I won't . . . !"

His mouth crushed down on hers, and he kissed her with a wild kind of frustration before he arched himself away from her and stood glaring down at her trembling body and wide misty eyes.

"Nothing's changed," he whispered huskily. "We cause a fever in each other so hot, ice couldn't quench it. Eventually you'll have me, Priscilla. Because the day will come when you can't bear the torture of wanting me any longer."

"But it won't last," she returned bitterly.

"Yes," he replied. "Yes, it will. You're all I see, hear, think, or need in all the world."

"It's just lust!" she threw at him. "You said so!"

He searched her wild eyes. "So I did. But it's much more than that," he said. "Much more. We must talk, and soon. I just wish I had the time now, but I don't. Good night, Priss."

He turned and walked away. It was several minutes before she could get her rubbery legs to take her back inside. And it was hours before she slept. She tossed and turned all

night long, worrying about John's dogged pursuit and her own vulnerability. What was she
going to do? She couldn't survive a second
rejection. Could she believe John when he
said the blazing passion between them would
last? It was a question to which she still
hadn't found an answer by morning.

She went with her parents to church and
then came back home and brooded for the rest
of the day. It was almost a relief when Monday morning came and she could go back to
school.

She heard from the twins that John was
frightfully busy, and her daydreams about
having him repeat his invitation to the muster
went up in smoke. Obviously he hadn't time
for anything else except the station right now.
And she couldn't even feel angry about it, now
that she knew what a difficult time he'd had
the past five years.

On Thursday the twins broke their record
streak of good behavior by putting a frog into
a little girl's dress. The ensuing pandemonium got Priscilla a stern lecture from
the principal, and she had to keep the twins
after class as punishment. They didn't
seem to mind and, secretly, neither did she.
She had a feeling that John would come for
them.

"Poor Uncle John's been staggering tired,"
Gerry told her that afternoon after the other
children had gone home.

"Dad offered to come home, but Uncle John said no," Bobby added. "He said that Mom and Dad needed . . . needed . . ." He frowned.

"A honeymoon," Gerry provided.

Priss laughed. "Well, I'm glad they're enjoying themselves. And I'm sure your uncle can cope."

"I say—" Ronald George stuck his head in the door—"your dad said to tell you that he and your mom are going to drive over to see the Thompsons and that they won't be home until about dark."

"Thanks, Ronald," she replied, grinning at him.

He seemed to take that as an invitation. He came into the room, shut the door, and perched his tall form on the edge of Priss's desk. His eyes went over the picture she made in her pale pink blouse and gray skirt.

"You look cool today," he remarked. "Like one of our English roses."

"Beware of my thorns," she teased mischievously.

"I'm not afraid of roses." He pursed his lips. He folded his arms. "As a matter of fact, I'm not afraid of anything today. I have scored a point."

She frowned and cast a quick look at the twins. But they were in the back of the room peering into the class's aquarium, where two turtles lived.

"Scored?" she questioned.

He leaned toward her, so that his face was almost touching hers. "Remember Mandy? Well, she's finally agreed to go out with me!"

She laughed softly. "Lucky old you!" she exclaimed. "Ronald, that's just super!"

"I can hardly wait," he continued, searching her twinkling eyes. "It must be love," he added more audibly.

To the man standing frozen and furious in the doorway, it was an eye-opening little tableau. Ronald leaning over Priss, with his mouth just inches from hers, and her bright face turned up and laughing at him, while he made her declarations of love. John clenched his hands by his side, weary from his day's work, his drill pants and bush shirt covered with dust and bits of wool and dirt, his face stern with anger.

Priss saw him first, and her heart turned over. "Oh. Hello, John," she faltered.

Ronald George straightened up, grinning. "Hi, Mr. Sterling. Nice day. You look a bit bushed."

"Down here, bushed means lost, and I'm not that," John returned with cold formality. "Gerry, Bobby, let's go."

He opened the door and ushered them out. And then he followed them! Without a word to Priss, without a single word, he was gone.

She couldn't help the sick, empty feeling in her stomach. She stared at the closed door with a sense of disaster. Surely he hadn't been jealous? She laughed bitterly to herself even as she thought it. John, jealous of her—that was a good one.

"I say, are you all right?" Ronald asked.

She forced a smile. "Of course. It's just been a long day. Well, I'd better pack up and go home. Thanks for the message. And good luck on your date!"

He stood up, smiling. "I'll need it. Mentally she can cut me to pieces. But she's a lovely lady, and I'm hopelessly smitten. Perhaps I can convince her I'm a good risk."

"I'm sure you will." Priss smiled at him. "See you tomorrow."

"Have a nice evening," he called as she went out the door with her belongings.

After she got home and changed, she walked down by the creek and sat there for a long time, puzzled over John's utter rudeness. Was he angry at her, or the boys, or had it just been weariness? Oh, how she wished she knew!

After a while, she took off her shoes and waded across the cool creek to the other side. She wandered up the small rise through the eucalyptus trees and saw the Sterling Run Land-Rover coming across the grassy paddock at a clip. Her heart leapt wildly when she recognized the driver.

Across the horizon were storm clouds, and even as John pulled up at the edge of the wooded area, rain started pelting down.

"Well, get in before you get wet," he growled, throwing open the passenger door.

She dived in, shoes in hand, and closed the door, scrutinizing him warily. He looked savage. His blue eyes glimmered under his heavy dark brows, and his lips made a thin line as he glared at her. He hadn't changed his clothing since she'd seen him at school, and he smelled of sheep and dust and the outdoors.

"Am I distasteful?" he asked curtly. "I'd forgotten how long it's been since you've seen me straight from the shearing sheds."

He wouldn't be distasteful to her if he were covered in tar and feathers, but she didn't say that. "You've been working hard, the boys said," she observed.

"Have to," he returned on a sigh as the rain came heavier, making of the cab a private, cozy haven. "We're still a long way from financial security at the station."

"You'll make it eventually," she said confidently.

He took off his hat and tossed it into the back of the vehicle, which was littered with tools and rags and dusty equipment. His hair was sweaty and he looked as ragged as he probably felt.

"What's going on between you and that pommy?" he inquired bluntly, pinning her with his eyes.

Her lips parted with an indrawn breath at

the unexpected attack. She lifted a hand to her hair and mussed it. "Nothing," she said.

"Don't hand me that," he growled. He threw a strong arm over the back of the seat, and she could see the muscles rippling under the darkly tanned skin. "He was making emphatic statements about being in love."

"Yes, but not with me," she burst out.

"There was no one else in the room, except the twins," he reminded her, glaring at her mouth.

Her breath caught in her throat, and she stared at his face with helpless longing. Her hands clenched in her lap, and she closed her eyes because she wanted so badly to kiss him. Outside the rain pelted the hood with a loud metallic sound.

"Oh, never mind," he said irritably. "Come here."

He held out one arm, and without really questioning her own docility, she went close to him, burrowing against his broad chest with a small contented sigh.

"I'll probably get you filthy, but I'm beyond caring," he murmured huskily as his arms contracted. "I'm starved for you, Priscilla." He nuzzled his face against hers and searched for her mouth. "Too starved."

She gave her mouth up to him, completely, letting him pierce the line of her lips with his tongue and penetrate to the soft darkness beyond. She didn't even protest when he turned her so she lay across his lap, or when he jerked open his shirt.

"Let me feel you," he whispered hungrily as his hand went to the buttons of her pink blouse. "All of you, against me, here . . ."

He had her mouth under his again, and her hands clung to his bare arms as he got the fabric out of the way and suddenly crushed her softness into the hard warm muscle and thick hair over his chest.

"Oh, God," he groaned huskily, folding her even closer. "Oh, God, how sweet, how sweet . . . !" He began to move her body so her breasts dragged against his skin, intensifying the need they were both feeling to such a degree that she cried out.

He lifted his shaggy head and looked into her eyes. His own were gleaming and wild. "Did I hurt you?" he asked shakily.

"No," she moaned. "Do it . . . do it again," she whispered.

He obliged, but this time he watched her face, watched the pleasure she was feeling as it was betrayed by her parted lips, her wide misty eyes.

His gaze dropped down to where their bodies met, and he watched the hard nipples disappear into the thick hair over his muscular chest.

"You are so beautiful," he breathed reverently. "Watching you . . . this way . . . drives me wild." He brought one hand from behind her and brushed his fingers lightly against the side of her breast. "Silk," he whispered as his fingers found the exquisite contours and then eased between their bodies to mold the peak.

His eyes shot back up to hers, and she lay helpless against him, trapped by the sensuality of his hands, his gaze. She was completely at his mercy, and he had to know it.

"I'll teach you to trust me somehow," he whispered, bending to her mouth. "Open your mouth, little virgin. All this . . . is only love-play. How could I take you in this damned dirty vehicle . . . ?"

That relaxed her a little. She didn't fight the possession of his mouth as he took her own again, a little more fervently this time.

"Honey, touch me," he coaxed. "Stroke me."

Her hands obeyed him. She liked the feel of his muscles, especially the ones just above his belt buckle. She touched him there, and he groaned, and the muscles clenched like coiled wire.

"Oh!" She stilled her fingers and looked up at him.

His lips were parted, swollen like her own, and he was having trouble breathing. His blond-streaked hair had fallen onto his brow, and he looked like a lover. Really like a lover.

"Do you feel adventurous?" he asked unsteadily. "Because if you do, I'll teach you some shocking things about a man's body."

Part of her was caught in the trap and wanted desperately to be taught. The saner part knew where all this was leading, and it was to a dead end. He only wanted her.

She leaned her forehead against him and pressed her hand flat over his heart. "No," she said in a defeated tone. "No, I can't; I can't go through it again," she murmured weakly. "I can't live through it twice. John, please, don't do this to me!"

His hands went to her back, and he held her close, feeling her breasts like satin against him, loving the bareness of her back, the scent of her.

He kissed her closed eyes, her forehead, in a breathlessly tender way and then eased her away from him.

His eyes went helplessly to her nakedness. She was bigger now, fuller, firmer, and the sight of her was glorious. It made his heart soar.

He reached out and ran a gentle finger over the swollen-tipped contours. "You were made for children," he breathed, thinking of how she'd look holding his.

Her whole body shook at the words, at the mental picture of a little blond baby suckling heartily at the place he was touching, and she stopped breathing as she met his level gaze.

It was like a moment out of time, when they were thinking the same thought, wanting the same thing. He bent his head and kissed her. And it was like no kiss they'd ever shared before. Tender, questioning. Full of wonder and shy exploration and aching softness.

He drew away and cupped her face in his hands to search her wide misty eyes. "Come and have supper at the Run tomorrow night," he invited quietly. "I'll cook."

Her mouth gaped. "Supper?"

"Yes. Only that." He reached down and pulled her clothing up, dressing her like a doll. "No more lovemaking for a while. I want to get to know you. What you feel. What you think. What you want from life."

Her body tingled. "Those are deep thoughts."

"Yes, aren't they." He fastened the top button of her blouse. "And in the meantime, it would help if you'd stop letting me undress you."

"I tried," she said with a faint smile.

He sighed. "Yes. I tried, too, but the feel of you does unexpected things to my brain. I'm sorry. I didn't mean for this to happen."

"It was so beautiful," she said without meaning to.

"Oh, God, yes," he ground out. He caught one of her hands and carried the palm reverently to his lips. "You've never done that sort of thing with anyone except me, have you?"

She shook her head. "I never wanted anyone else's hands . . ." She bit her lip and lowered her eyes.

He tilted her eyes up to his. "Neither did I," he said.

She searched that weathered face pensively, curiously.

His finger brushed the line of her lips. "I haven't slept with a woman in five years."

It was like a jolt of electricity going through her body. Her eyes dilated, and she gaped at him. "Five years?"

He nodded. "So you see, there's been no one else for me, either, Priscilla."

Tears bled from her eyes. She couldn't help them. "But you're a man," she whispered.

"I didn't feel like much of a man after the way I cut you up," he confessed, handing her a clean handkerchief. "I had a mental block about sex. I even tried once." He laughed mirthlessly. "She wasn't an understanding woman, and that made it worse. She laughed."

She went into his arms and held him, burying her face in his neck. "Who was she?" she ground out. "I'll kill her!"

His arms contracted. "Jealous?"

"Furious. How could she do that to you?"

He drew in a slow breath. "You're still very innocent in some ways," he reminded her.

"I'd never do that," she said fervently.

"I know. If I were totally impotent, I imagine you'd find some way to make me feel like a man again, wouldn't you?"

She lifted her face and looked into his eyes. He understood the question there.

"No," he responded softly. "I'm not impotent. Not with you."

She smiled shyly and lowered her eyes to his chest.

"If you'd like me to prove it," he offered, "I'd be only too glad to oblige."

This was the old teasing John Sterling she remembered from her teens, the man she'd worshipped and grown to love. Not the distant stranger of past weeks and years. It must have been a barren life for him, if he'd had no one since Janie Weeks. Janie. Her eyes clouded. She wanted desperately to ask him about the divorcée, to ask if it had hurt when she deserted him. Did he still feel anything for Janie? But she was too unsure of him to ask such a personal question. Instead she forced her eyes up to his and smiled softly.

"What would you do if I said yes, go ahead?" she asked.

He chuckled softly. "I'd find some excuse to go home. I don't want to take your virginity in the front seat of a Land-Rover, if it's all the same to you. I'm too old for impatient groping."

Her eyes measured the size of the seat and the size of his body and she laughed softly. "No, I guess it would be impossible."

"Sweet innocent," he sighed, touching his mouth to hers, "we could do it sitting up, didn't you know?"

She flushed from her hairline down to her breasts, and he looked at her and laughed so delightedly, she couldn't even get angry.

"I'll drive you home, darling," he said gently. "I don't want you catching cold."

He moved her beside him but held her arm when she tried to go back to her own side of the vehicle.

"No," he protested. "Stay close."

She didn't argue. She pressed herself against his side and closed her eyes and rested her cheek on his stained shirt with a soulful sigh.

His arm contracted as he started the vehicle and put it in gear with his free hand. "I've ruined your blouse," he remarked as he pulled back onto the track.

"I don't mind," she answered.

"When we do this again, I'll make sure I've cleaned up first. I went off half cocked about your pommy friend and didn't even consider how I looked," he laughed.

"You were looking for me?" she asked.

He chuckled softly. "I thought I'd probably find you at the creek. You spend quite a lot of time brooding there, don't you?"

"I like to watch the birds."

He kissed her forehead lightly. "Yes, I know."

It took only a few short minutes to get to her parents' home, and she drew away from him with all-too-obvious reluctance.

"I meant what I said," he repeated. "No more lovemaking for a while. We're going to learn about each other in less physical ways."

That was promising and rather exciting. She smiled at him with a little of her old spirit. "Afraid I might seduce you, John?" she teased gently.

He caught her hand and held it to his lips. "Yes," he admitted, and he didn't smile. "And deathly afraid I might seduce you. So we'll cool it for a while. All right?"

"All right." She glanced at him one last time and got out of the Land-Rover. He studied her warmly for a long minute.

"What was the pommy telling you?" he asked finally.

She grinned at him. "That he had a date with the girl he's dying of love for, and how happy he was."

He grimaced. "Well, as long as he's not after you, I suppose he's safe enough. I'll pick you up about six tomorrow."

"I could drive over—" she began.

"I'll pick you up about six," he returned firmly. "I don't want you on the roads alone at night."

He backed out of the driveway before she could make any remarks about being liberated and able to take care of herself. And as she went inside she couldn't help thinking how nice it felt to be cared for, protected. But what was he after now? He'd said he didn't want to seduce her. Did that mean that he was beginning to feel something for her after all? Her heart raced wildly. Her eyes closed. And if he was, did she dare take the risk a second time? That nagging thought weighed on her mind all night.

Chapter Eleven

$\mathscr{I}$t was an unexpected treat to find the twins, as well as John, dressed to the hilt when they all came to get Priscilla the next evening. She was wearing the same white gauzy creation she'd worn several nights before, and John admired it.

"I like that," he complimented.

She grinned. "I haven't gone shopping in quite a while, so it will just have to do."

"Have fun, darling," Renée said from the door.

"We'll have her home by midnight," John promised as he helped her into the Ford.

"Dinkum, we will!" Gerry called out the window.

Priss looked over the backseat at the terrible twins. Gerry was wearing a blue suit, Bobby a brown one, and they did look elegant.

"I'd never have believed it," she told them with pursed lips. "You're both very handsome."

"Uncle John is, too, isn't he?" Gerry pressed her.

She surveyed John as he climbed in the front seat. He was dressed in a tan safari suit, his head was bare, and he looked as rugged as the country he lived in.

"Yes, he is," Priss commented absently, studying him. "Very handsome, indeed."

He lifted an eyebrow and smiled at her. "Thank you, Miss Johnson," he responded dryly. "I must say, you look lovely yourself."

She smiled back and started to settle herself on the seat, when he laid his big arm over the back of it and stared at her.

"Come here, love," he said in a voice that made her toes curl.

She eased closer without a single protest and felt the reassuring warmth and strength of his body with surging delight.

"That's more like it," he murmured as he started the Ford and eased it into gear. "Tell Priss what we're having for supper, boys," he called into the backseat.

"We're having steak and salad!" Gerry said.

"And apple pie for afters," Bobby added.

"And homemade rolls!" Gerry interrupted. "Uncle John did them all alone!"

"When I was a boy, the cook we hired on for the shearing gang used to go on benders at the damndest times," he explained as they drove toward the Run in the moonlit darkness. "I learned to pinch-hit in self-defense." He looked down at her. "Men work harder when they've been fed."

"Do they?" she questioned, smiling up at him.

His arm tightened, and she sighed. Minutes later he pulled up in front of the Colonial-style house and the boys piled out quickly, racing for the porch.

John helped Priss get out and then stiffened at the haunting doglike howl that echoed beyond the outbuildings.

"A dingo," he growled.

"But doesn't the dingo fence keep them out?" she asked, recalling the miles and miles of fence around the sheep-raising country in the state of Queensland, along the New South Wales border and into western Australia. It was something of an international legend.

"Not entirely," he informed her. "We still have to hunt them down occasionally."

She shivered as the sound came again.

"They rarely attack people," he told her, drawing her close at his side. "Besides, love, I'd never let anything hurt you."

"Yes, I know," she murmured. She let her eyes half close as they walked. Those were the sweetest steps she'd taken in five long years.

In no time, they were seated at the long elegant dinner table Mrs. Sterling had imported from England, enjoying the succulent steak John had cooked.

"You're very good at this," Priss praised when they'd worked their way through to the apple pie.

"Necessity," he explained with a smile. "I can think of things I'd rather do than cook."

"How's your mother?" Priss asked then.

"Doing very well. She tells me she's dating a financier." He glanced up. "I expect she may marry him."

"Will you mind?"

He shook his head. "She's entitled to some happiness."

"Uncle John, can we be excused?" Gerry asked as he finished off his apple pie. "There's this dinkum movie on about the outback . . ."

"Go ahead," John told them. "Don't put the volume up too loud, though," he added.

"Sure!" Bobby agreed. "We'll be quiet as mice," he promised as they rushed off into the living room.

"They've changed a lot in the past week," Priss noted.

"Yes, I've seen it. I think when Randy and Latrice work out their problems, things will be better all around." He sat back with a glass of white wine he'd just poured, and sipped it casually. "Did you mean what you told me the other day—that you were planning to go back to Hawaii?"

She studied the tablecloth. "At the time, I did."

"And now? After yesterday?"

She looked up into his serene, steady gaze and felt her heart do cartwheels in her chest. "I don't know that I could leave now."

He searched her eyes for a long moment. Then he put the wineglass down. "Do you feel you could live in Australia for the rest of your life, without regretting it?"

"I planned that from the day my family came here," she said, curious about where the conversation was heading.

But he changed the subject abruptly. "How does your father like having you at the school with him?"

She laughed. "He likes it a lot. He says now he has someone to sit with at lunch. I love my parents," she related quietly. "They've been everything to me."

"I'm rather fond of them myself," he concurred.

"John, what was your father like?" she asked as she sipped her own wine.

He shrugged. "I'm not sure. All I have is my mother's memory of him. And she worshipped the ground he walked on." He stared blankly at his wineglass. "I was only a toddler when he died. Randy was newborn. Neither of us ever knew him. He was killed by a brumby."

"That's a wild horse, isn't it?"

"Yes." He put the glass down. "I've often wondered how things might have gone if he'd lived. Randy and I were never close, until this crisis came up. Mother . . ." He laughed. "You know Mother. She likes her independence. I grew up not liking ties. It's been hard for me to change. To get used to the idea of answering to another human being."

She supposed he meant to Randy, since his brother had taken over the station. She put down her wineglass and dabbed at her full lips with the napkin.

"I suppose it was the other way with me," she replied. "I was loved and indulged and protected. Oh, my parents disciplined me along the way, but I was never allowed to learn things by experience."

"Except with me," he mused, watching her.

She smiled slowly. "Except with you." She looked up into his broad tanned face wonderingly. "Why did you put up with me?"

"You were a beautiful girl," he said simply. "Like sunshine to be around. Full of life and joy and delightful warmth. I enjoyed being with you, even before I discovered what it was like to want you in any physical way."

"Did you want me before that afternoon I left for college?" she queried, but she couldn't manage to meet his eyes as she asked the question.

"Remember the morning you came running across the paddock barefoot?" he asked, smiling at the memory. "To show me the scholarship you'd won?"

"Yes," she said.

"That was the first time. I looked at you and had a sudden, and rather frightening, reaction to you." He stroked his wineglass as if it were a woman's body, but he was looking across the table at Priss. "I was trying to decide what to do about it when you started avoiding me." His eyes fell to the table. "I didn't quite know how to handle that. It disturbed me greatly."

She felt her nerves tingle with pleasure as she studied his broad chest. He looked up then, his eyes mysterious and vividly blue in his craggy face as he viewed her.

"Then I came out to the house to ask why, to say good-bye. And I kissed you." His eyebrows lifted, and he smiled wickedly. "It was meant to be just a kiss, for good-bye. But once I started, you see, I found that I couldn't stop. You never knew that it was touch and go with me, did you, Priss?" he added meaningfully. "All that saved you was the fear that I might make you pregnant."

"Terrifying thought!" she murmured, trying to make light of it.

"Not at all," he countered quietly. "I found myself considering children. And ties. And settling down. And that was when I decided to go to Hawaii and ask you to marry me." He pushed his chair back. "And then the bottom fell out."

She didn't like thinking about that. She heard him come around the table to pull her chair out.

"Let's go sit in my study," he suggested. "I could use a brandy, and the boys won't disturb us in there."

She got up, her eyes involuntarily going to his face.

"No," he breathed, looking back with equal urgency. "We can't. Sure as hell they'd walk in on us, and I don't want them asking embarrassing questions."

She flushed. "I wasn't—" she protested.

"I want it, too," he ground out. He was standing close enough that the warmth of his body warmed hers, too. He smelled of spicy cologne and soap.

She drew in a steadying breath. "I'm sorry."

"There's nothing to be sorry about. Come on." He caught her hand in his and locked his fingers into hers. Big warm fingers, very strong, very capable. She felt lighter than air as he led her along with him. "I missed you," he confided. "For five years, I didn't spend a night without thinking about where you were, what you were doing. Who you were with."

She'd done that, too, but she wasn't going to admit it. Her pride had taken a hell of a blow already.

"It must have been very hard for you, at first," she prodded. "Losing the station, I mean."

"Yes. It cut my pride to ribbons. And Randy had a bit of a superiority complex at the outset. That didn't help, either." He tightened his grip on her hand. "I was devastated at first. I all but gave up. There was so little left to lose that I stopped giving a damn." He led her into the study, leaving the door open, and left her at the couch while he poured brandy into two snifters. "Then Randy got in over his head and came to me for advice. A first," he added with a faint grin. "I got caught up in the challenge, and we've been working well together ever since."

She stared down at her folded hands. "So everything worked out for the best, anyway."

"Not quite." He handed her a snifter and dropped down beside her with his in hand. "I lost you."

"Was that so bad? You didn't seem to think so at the time."

"Someday, at a better time, I'll tell you all about it. But not tonight." He slid an arm around her. "Come close, love. Tell me about Hawaii."

She kicked off her shoes and curled up in the curve of his arm, loving the warm contact. Her head rested on his shoulder and she nuzzled against him.

"There isn't a lot to tell. I studied hard. I had friends. I went on weekend trips to the other islands, and once I flew to California for summer vacation. I had a marvelous time, but I missed Australia."

"You never came home, did you?" he probed.

She smiled sadly. "I was afraid I might see you."

He shifted restlessly. "But the pommy was always around, wasn't he?"

"Ronald was my best friend," she confirmed. "I'm very fond of him. He was there when I needed someone to cry on. But it was only friendship."

"I thought you loved him," he said.

She shook her head, feeling the hard muscle of his arm behind her nape. "No. Not even at first."

"Did you miss me?" he quizzed after a minute. "Or were you too bitter?"

"I was bitter at first. But I got over it," she lied. "Then I tried not to think about you."

"Successfully?"

She bit her lower lip. "Sometimes."

His fingers curved under her chin and nudged it up so he could search her wide, sad green eyes. He caressed the side of her throat with a light pressure that made her pulse go crazy.

"I'd think of you at night sometimes," he said. "And it would get so bad, I'd climb into my clothes and saddle a horse and ride for hours. And when I got back, tired to the bone and half dead from lack of sleep, I'd lie awake and remember how it felt to cherish your mouth under mine."

Her lower lip trembled, because it had been that way with her, too.

"I missed you so badly," he whispered gruffly, bending. "It was like losing part of me."

His mouth pressed down against hers, cool and moist and tasting of brandy. He kissed her tenderly, lovingly, breaking the taut line of her lips with a lazy coaxing pressure that soon became slow and deep and urgent.

She made a tiny sound in her throat and turned to get closer to him.

"Wait a minute," he whispered. He stopped long enough to get the brandy snifters out of the way, and then she was in his arms, held close, crushed against his shirt. He kissed her so deeply, that she felt her heart turn over in her breast.

He groaned deeply, forcing her head into the curve of his elbow with the urgency of his need.

She touched his cheek, ran her fingers into

his hair. She moaned softly as one big hand moved under her arm and began to lightly stroke the soft flesh there.

"Yes," she murmured eagerly, moving her body to tempt his fingers onto it.

"No," he ground out, lifting his head. He was breathing roughly, and his eyes devoured her, but he put her away from him. "No more. I can't handle this."

He got to his feet, running his fingers through his blond-streaked hair, breathing heavily. His back was to her as he stared out the darkened window and stretched to ease the tension in his body.

She sat up, gnawing her lip, wondering at his self-control.

"You always could do that," she commented on a nervous laugh.

He turned, frowning. "Do what?"

"Pull away. Stop before things got out of control." Her eyes fell. "I was never able to draw back."

"You were an innocent. I wasn't." He laughed softly. "And I had plenty of practice controlling my urges when I was with you. All I had to do was hum Brahms's lullaby to myself."

"I might not have gotten pregnant," she argued.

"I'd have bet the station on it," he returned shortly. His eyes searched hers, and he smiled. "Did you expect that I'd have stopped with one time?"

Her lips parted on a surprised breath. "Wouldn't you?" she asked in a whisper.

He shook his head from side to side. "Three or four times by morning, darling," he said quietly. "At least."

Her face flamed. "I always thought . . . men gave out."

"You've got a lot to learn. And someday soon," he added with an intent stare, "I'm going to teach you all of it."

She steeled herself to refuse. "I won't have an affair with you—I've already said that."

"I know." He moved back to the sofa and sat down beside her. His face was solemn as he drew a box out of the pockets of his bush jacket and pressed it into her hands. "Open that when you get home. I'll come for you first thing in the morning, and we'll talk."

She touched the gray felt of the small box lightly, her eyes conveying her puzzlement.

"Don't open it until you get home," he repeated. He bent and kissed her mouth tenderly. "And don't worry yourself to death about my motives. Think about what life will be like without me. Because I've already considered that question. And I've decided that no life at all would be better than living without you."

She hardly heard anything else he said for the rest of the evening. She was still in a daze when he took her home, and she mumbled something to the boys, forgot to say anything at all to John, and went into her house at ten o'clock feeling as if she'd been out all night.

It wasn't until she was in bed that she opened the tiny box with trembling fingers and looked at its contents. It was a blazing emerald, small but perfect, in a gold setting. The engagement ring was accompanied by a solid-gold band with the same intricate design. She watched it blur before her eyes and only then realized that she was crying.

All the long years she'd loved John Sterling, she'd never imagined how it might feel if he bought her a ring. He hadn't when he'd proposed in Hawaii; he hadn't even mentioned buying a ring. And now here it was, without the proposal, and she didn't think she had enough strength in her body to turn him down.

For better or for worse, for richer or for poorer . . . she didn't mind that he wasn't rich. She'd work beside him. She'd take care of him. And at night she'd sleep in his big arms. And in time would come children. Then perhaps he'd grow to love her. Perhaps the physical need he had of her would grow into an emotional one and what she felt for him would be returned.

There was, though, the chance that it wouldn't. Yet when she thought about living the rest of her life without him, it was a chance she was willing to take. She knew there'd never be another man. She didn't want anyone else. She hadn't in five years.

Her fingers trembled as she took the emerald out and slid it onto her wedding finger, finding the fit perfect. Her eyes closed in a silent prayer. This time it had to work. This time she had to make him love her. It was already too late to run away. She was more deeply in love than she had been at eighteen. Too much in love to let go.

Chapter Twelve

Naturally Priss didn't sleep all night. She climbed out of bed at five A.M. with bloodshot eyes and tugged on a frilly long white robe over her blue pajamas before she dragged herself to the kitchen to start breakfast.

Her parents were still asleep, and she felt as if she were sleepwalking herself. She yawned as she put the biscuits she'd just rolled out into the oven and started the coffee.

A noise in the yard caught her attention. It sounded very much like a car engine, but surely John wouldn't be here at five in the morning . . .

She opened the door and he came up the back steps into the house. He looked as tired as she felt. He was wearing his work clothing, pale drill trousers with a khaki bush shirt and the slouch hat he wore to work cattle. He took off the hat and closed the door and stared down at her with eyes so blue and piercing, they made her heart race.

"I couldn't wait any longer," he explained softly, searching her sleepy face. "I've hardly slept."

"Me, too," she returned.

He tossed his hat onto the counter and sighed. "Well?"

She felt shy with him. Eighteen all over again and half afraid of his formidable masculinity. Instead of answering him, she held out her left hand, where the emerald ring sparkled with green fire in the kitchen light.

His breath caught. His eyes closed. "Thank God," he uttered. And he reached for her.

She held him as hard as he was holding her, overwhelmed by the pleasure of belonging to him at last.

"I've never wanted anything so much," he breathed over her head, rocking her gently in his enveloping arms. "No regrets, Priss?"

She drew in a slow breath, and all the old doubts gnawed at her for a minute. "Not . . . regrets, no. But . . ." She drew back to look up into his tanned face. "John, you're sure this time?"

His face hardened as he read the uncertainty and fear of rejection that lay naked in her pale green eyes.

"If it's any consolation, what I did to you will haunt me all my life," he replied quietly. "Yes, I'm sure this time. No, I'm not going to back out at the last minute. We're going to get married and live together and build a life for ourselves."

Her eyes misted, and she smiled wobbily at him. "Gee, that sounds nice," she whispered. "I feel all eighteen and nervous again."

His fingers touched her disheveled hair, and his eyes ran over her with possession in their twinkling depths. "You look about that this morning," he agreed with a warm smile. "I didn't know you liked pajamas."

She smiled. "I can wear nightgowns after we're married, if you like."

"I'd like it better if you don't wear anything at all," he teased. "I don't."

Her face colored, and he seemed to like that. He bent and touched her mouth lazily with his. "You belong to me now," he whispered, and lifted her high in his arms. "That's better. You're short without shoes."

"Because you're so big."

"I'll take care of you, Priss," he promised, searching her eyes. "We won't have a lot, but I'll try to ensure you never regret marrying me."

She studied his hard face with loving eyes. At least he was willing to commit himself this far, she thought. Perhaps love would come eventually.

"I'll never regret it," she promised, meaning it. She tugged his head down to hers and kissed him softly, slowly, savoring the very texture of his hard lips. His arms contracted. She felt his chest crushing her breasts gently, felt the long powerful line of his legs against hers and moaned, clinging to his broad shoulders.

They were so lost in each other, they didn't hear the door open, or see the stunned, then delighted look that Adam and Renée exchanged.

"Ahem!" Renée grinned.

They broke apart, looking guilty, and then John started laughing.

"It isn't quite as bad as it looks," he said with a wicked glance at Priss, who was clinging to his side. "I haven't been here all night."

"I don't know about that," Adam gibed with a mischievous smile. "You both look guilty as sin to me."

"Yes, they do, don't they?" Renée added fondly.

"Actually, we've been sealing our engagement," John volunteered.

Priss held out her hand, and her eyes were the same fiery sparkling emerald as the stone. "We're going to be married," she said in a voice that was husky with feeling. She was sure her feet were floating above the floor.

After that was pandemonium. It wasn't until they were all sitting at the table eating breakfast that there was a break in the conversation.

"Well, when is the wedding?" Adam inquired.

"As soon as I can get a license," John said firmly, glancing at Priss. "I've waited five years. I won't wait any longer."

"That suits me very well," Priss added. "We can be married here, can't we, Mom?"

Renée was staring blankly at her daughter. "Here?"

"Well, yes. Just the minister and all of us and maybe Randy and Latrice . . . ?"

Renée let her breath out. "It sounds just like us, doesn't it, darling?" she addressed Adam, laughing. "We did the same thing, you know. It's better than a large wedding, really; much less anxiety."

"Also much quicker." Adam grinned at John.

John grinned back. "We're both so old, we need all the time we can get; don't we, darling?" he added, winking at Priss.

"Speak for yourself, old fossil," she told him as she dug into her scrambled eggs. "I'm a mere child, myself."

"That's no way to talk to your future husband," John chided sternly.

"Excuse me, darling," she cooed, relishing the word as she peeked at him through her lashes. "You just give the orders, and I'll ignore them. All right?"

John sighed. "I can see that we're going to have to have a long talk about some of the finer details of marriage."

"Okay," Priss agreed. She laid down her fork. "What would you like to know?"

He threw back his head and laughed. "I've done myself in!"

She only smiled. "Yes, darling," she replied seductively, and batted her eyelashes at him. "Lucky, lucky you!"

He didn't laugh then. He just searched her face with soft intent eyes. "Luckier than you know," he responded. "I'll check on the license today," he added, dragging his eyes back to Adam and Renée.

Priss just stared at him, her gaze so full of love that Renée had to drop her eyes.

The next two weeks seemed to go by in a flurry of activity, as Priss tried to balance work and daydreaming, and being with John every evening.

He didn't press his advantage, now that they were totally committed to each other. He was more friend than lover, and they talked to each other as never before. She learned that he liked classical music, and he learned that she was an old-motion-picture fanatic. They discovered mutual interests in ballet and opera and art. And every day she grew to love him more. All her doubts and uncertainties slowly faded as she realized that nothing was going to stop the wedding this time.

He surprised her by phoning Margaret and having a wedding dress identical to the one she'd chosen five years before flown in from Hawaii. It was a measure of the regard he felt for her, she saw, and she felt a fleeting regret that he couldn't love her as she loved him. But at least he liked her, she consoled herself, and after they had children, surely he'd grow fonder of her.

The ceremony was held at Priss's home, and Randy and Latrice were there as well as Ronald George and Betty Gaines. Even the twins were invited, and they astounded the assembled company with perfect textbook etiquette. Latrice and Randy looked like newlyweds themselves, and Latrice was actually sitting with her sons, hugging them, before the ceremony began.

Ronald George came forward to offer his congratulations, extending his hand warily to John as if he expected it would be instantly removed. But John didn't say an unkind word. He only smiled.

Minutes later the ceremony began, and Priss clutched her small wildflower bouquet in her hand as they stood before the minister and the words of the marriage service were spoken.

When the minister came to the part about speaking now or forever holding your peace,

Priss froze. She darted a glance up at John, all her old fears haunting her. But he looked down at her and smiled slowly, softly, and she relaxed.

He slid the wedding band that matched her engagement ring onto her finger and repeated the appropriate words with so much feeling that Priss felt tears sting her eyes. When she added her own part, and the minister concluded the ceremony, tears were rolling unashamedly down her cheeks.

She kept her eyes open as John bent to kiss her, and so did he. She thought there had never been a more beautiful time in her entire life. For so many years she'd worshipped him, and now he was her husband. He belonged to her.

"Don't cry," he whispered, lifting his mouth. "This is only the beginning. The best is yet to come."

She tried to smile, and he kissed her wet eyelids closed. They were surrounded by wellwishers during the next few minutes, and in the excitement of cutting the cake and changing into her beige traveling suit and saying good-bye to her parents, there was no time to think.

Minutes later they drove away in John's Ford, waving good-bye. They would spend the night in Brisbane before boarding a plane to Hawaii the next morning for a brief honeymoon. A substitute teacher had been engaged to fill Priss's place for the few days that John could afford to be away from the station.

"Next year, I'll take you to the States," he promised as they drove away.

"I don't mind if we never go anywhere, as long as we're together," she said quietly. She squeezed the fingers that he had imprisoned on his thigh and leaned her head against his shoulder.

"Five years," he said unexpectedly, and his eyes were stormy. His jaw was clenched, making the dimple more prominent. He looked formidable at that moment, and Priss stared at him uneasily.

"What's wrong?" she asked. "Are you sorry that we—"

"No!" He glanced at her quickly, then dragged his eyes back to the road. He lifted her hand to his mouth and kissed it softly. "I'm only sorry that we wasted so many years because of my damned black pride, that's all."

"Maybe it was for the best," she said gently. "I was very young."

"You still are, in all the ways that count. You make me feel like celebrating every time you smile at me," he said unexpectedly.

"In that case, I'll smile a lot," she promised. Her eyes searched his profile dreamily. "I used to hide and watch you when you'd ride the fence line," she mused. "I thought you were the handsomest man on earth."

"Did you?" he chuckled.

"I still do. There was never anyone who compared with you, in all those years." Her eyes dropped to his white collar and missed the look of love on his face. "Eventually I gave up looking."

"I'm glad of that," he acknowledged quietly. "I used to have nightmares about hearing that you'd married someone in Hawaii."

"Did you really?" she asked. Her eyes fell. "I had the same nightmares about you and Janie Weeks."

There was a long poignant silence. "We'll talk about that when we get to the hotel in Brisbane," he said then. "It's time, past time, that we cleared the air about Janie. And a few other things." He studied her intently. "Turn on the radio, will you, love?"

She tuned in a pop channel and snuggled close to him. All the rest of the way, not one word broke into the music. She closed her eyes, pretending he loved her.

They arrived in Brisbane about dusk and checked into an exclusive hotel on the beach. John had said that this one luxury would have to last a long time, but she didn't mind. Anywhere with John was heaven: she wouldn't have minded camping on the beach in a tent.

Once they got upstairs, she took advantage of the huge whirlpool tub to soak away the tiredness of the long day. She'd had some wild idea that her wedding night would be conventional. That John would take her out to supper, bring her back to the room, and that then their married life would begin. But knowing John, she should have expected what happened.

She was lying in the enormous bathtub, surrounded by soap bubbles, enjoying the soft gyration of the water as the whirlpool jetted currents all around her in its gentlest cycle. Her eyes were closed, and she didn't hear a sound until the bathroom door suddenly closed.

She opened her eyes, and John cocked an eyebrow at her wild blush. She was startled to see him nude as she was, bronzed skin rippling under the dark blond hair that covered his broad chest, muscular stomach, flat hips, and long powerful legs.

"You might as well get used to me," he murmured. "I'm not going to spend our married life undressing in closets, and I sleep like this." He tossed his robe over the vanity chair. "Feel like company in there?" He nodded toward the tub.

She swallowed. It was all happening so fast. He's my husband, she told herself firmly. We're married. I have to forget all my hangups now; it's all right to sleep with him.

"Yes," she managed in a strangled voice. Her eyes measured him. "Is the tub going to be big enough?" she asked.

He searched her eyes. "Yes. More than adequate for what I have in mind, Mrs. Sterling."

She moved over, watching him approach, long-legged, slim-hipped, powerfully built. He was the most beautiful thing she'd ever seen— even more sensuous than the Greek statues that had fascinated her in school.

"This is kinky," she commented impishly as he eased down into the tub with her.

"Why?" he asked.

The contact with his long bare body was doing frightening things to her nerves. Her whole body tensed deliciously as she felt his powerful thigh against hers, as his arm went around her shoulders and she felt its warm weight.

"Bathing together?" she laughed.

He looked down at her with amused eyes. "Don't you like it? The government will be delighted that we're saving water."

"Yes, I suppose so." The soap bubbles hid most of her from his curious eyes, and vice versa, but she was still blushing. "Oh, John, I've got the most horrible hang-ups about sex," she blurted out, and turned to bury her face against the wet mat of hair over his chest.

He chuckled softly, holding her there. "Why?"

"I don't know anything, and I'm afraid," she answered. She looked up at his broad face with its firm lips and twinkling eyes and dimpled chin. "John, you aren't going to hurt me, are you?"

He brushed the damp hair away from her face. "I'll try not to. I don't think it's going to be so difficult. All virgins don't have a rough time." He bent and kissed her mouth tenderly. "You know I've been a long time without a woman," he reminded her. "Is that what frightens you? Are you afraid I may go wild in your arms?"

She touched his chest nervously. "You're so strong . . ."

"And so intent on pleasing you," he countered amusedly. "It may not be heaven the first time, but if it isn't, I'll more than make it up to you by morning. Now relax."

"We aren't going to . . . in here, are we?" she hesitated, wide-eyed.

His hand slid over her shoulder, against one full hard-tipped breast, down her waist and her flat stomach and the silken skin of her inner thigh. "Why not, love?" he asked, letting his eyes hold hers as his hand moved with expert precision on her soft body.

She gasped, and he took the soft sound into his mouth as he kissed her for the first time with total possession. She stiffened a little, but seconds later she yielded to him, and he felt her fingers grasping helplessly at his arms.

He turned her, knocking the drain with his

foot so that some of the water seeped out while he was kissing her senseless. He touched her lovingly with expert, seeking hands, exploring the satin of her skin, the tender innocence of her body.

"I'm glad," he breathed roughly as his head went to her slippery breasts. "Oh, God, I'm so glad you kept yourself for me, that I'm your first man."

Tears welled up in her eyes at the sharp, sweet twinges of pleasure he was causing. "So . . . am I," she moaned. Her teeth bit at his shoulder, and she began to move, not because she wanted to, but because she couldn't help it. He was making her feel things that shocked, frightened, fascinated her. Priss's eyes opened wide as he did something new and intimate to her body.

She cried out, and he lifted his head.

"It's all right," he whispered, shifting so he was above her. His eyes held hers. "Relax for me. Just relax. We'll go at your pace, so don't be frightened, darling."

And all at once, before she had time to be afraid, he was making her a part of his own body. Her eyes dilated, and she started to stiffen, but he stroked her and smiled down at her. His own lack of urgency, his evident self-control, made it possible for her not to fight him. She let her body sink in the water with a breathless little sigh.

His large hand under her hips lifted her

gently. "You see?" he soothed. "It's not going to be difficult, is it?"

"I didn't think—" She couldn't manage to tell him what she didn't think, because he moved unexpectedly, and she saw stars. Her breath caught in her throat as his hips shifted and she clung wildly to him, really frightened of the sensations that were making her shudder helplessly.

His mouth eased over hers, and just before he took total possession, he looked straight into her eyes.

"Now," he whispered shakily, as the hunger and need and newness of being with her took his control. "Now we'll make up for all the long, lost years. We'll make them up here, now, together. . . . God, Priss, love me!" he groaned against her mouth, and his big body shuddered with fierce need. His fingers dug into her slender hips, lifting her. And it began. She almost fainted as he brought her to the precipice and let her back down again, only to start once more, arousing her and calming her, over and over, until at last there was no coming down from the peak.

She clung and wept and shivered, hearing his rough breathing suddenly stop just before a harsh cry burst from his lips. She felt him shudder, too, and only then realized what was happening. And by that time, it was happening to her, too, and she gave her mind up to it.

They lay together in the churning water,

clinging, kissing softly, tenderly, as the trembling passed and their heartbeats calmed at last. He brushed back her wet hair and gave a low triumphant laugh.

"This is one memory we'll never share with our children," he murmured devilishly. "That we came together for the first time in a whirlpool bathtub filled with bubbles."

She kissed his shoulder and snuggled against him, loving the feel of his body. "I love you."

"Yes, I know. I've always known. That was what made it so very difficult to let you go."

Her fingers traced a slow pattern in the hair over his heart. "I guess I was pretty obvious," she murmured.

"That much love is hard to hide," he said tenderly. His hand smoothed her hair. "It was all that kept me going sometimes—knowing that you hadn't stopped loving me."

"How did you know that?" she asked curiously.

"Renée told me."

"My mother sold me out?" she exclaimed, lifting her head.

His eyes were solemn. "There was a time, only once, when I was ready to do something drastic. I thought of selling the station to Randy and joining the service. When Renée found out, she told me." He kissed her eyes closed. "I lived on it," he breathed huskily. "I lived on it for years! Then you came home, and it was so difficult to get close to you again. I was sure you hated me. Then when Randy told you the truth, I was terrified that it was pity you felt. When I told you I only wanted your body, it was because I was hurting. It wasn't true." He kissed her mouth slowly, passionately. "Only later, when I started asking myself why you had stayed a virgin all those years, did the pieces fall into place. That was when I decided I still had a chance. And I went after you with every weapon I could find."

Her heart pounded heavily, and he felt it, because his hand was cupping her breast.

He lifted his head and rolled over, so that her body was resting atop his. His hands smoothed up and down her back while his eyes grew drunk on her pink bareness. "Priss, it was never only physical, except maybe for that afternoon in your bedroom. After that, it was an obsession that got completely out of hand; that took over my very soul. I came to Hawaii after you because I was dying without you."

Tears sprang to her eyes. "You loved me?"

"Darling," he breathed roughly, "I still do. I always have; always will. Otherwise do you think I'd have been celibate for five damned years? Didn't that give me away?"

She stared at him blankly. "I never dreamed—"

"Greenhorn," he chided, "it's nothing short

of sainthood for a man to go that long without sex!"

"Oh," she exclaimed. Her eyes searched his. "But . . . but there was Janie Weeks . . ." she began hoarsely, and the pain wrenched her.

His arms folded her gently against him in the warm water, and he sighed bitterly. "I never touched her," he said at last, feeling her stiffen with shock. "That's right, never. Oh, we went out enough times, and I'll admit that I hoped at first she would take my mind off you. But I never saw her again after I got back from Hawaii. I didn't even want to."

"But why?" she ground out. "Why did you tell me that lie? And my parents—they told me you were seeing her, too."

"I made them promise to back up my story," he said quietly. "Because I knew the fiction of another woman was the only way I could keep you from rushing back here and sacrificing yourself for me."

"I loved you," she wept. "It wouldn't have been a sacrifice!"

"Inevitably it would," he corrected, his voice even. "You were too young to cope with it all. I couldn't risk having your feeling for me turn to hatred in the face of all the obstacles. Remember, Priss, I wasn't even sure I could salvage the station at all. My pride was in the dust. And as it was, I had to go to work for Randy. That was rough. It changed me."

"I knew you'd changed, yes. I just didn't understand why. And I hated you for Janie." Tears ran down her cheeks onto his hairy chest. "Oh, John," she wailed. "Five years. Five long years, and I grieved for you so!"

His arms tightened around her. "So did I, for you," he confessed under his breath. "Ached for you, hungered for you! There was never another woman. My God, how could there have been? After the first time I kissed you, I couldn't have touched anyone else."

"You said you tried," she reminded him.

"Yes. When I thought you and that pommy were going to make a match of it. That was before I spoke to Renée." He sighed. "I stayed drunk two days after I tried, Priscilla. I felt as if I'd tried to commit adultery."

She smiled wobbily. Her fingers traced patterns on his chest. "John, could you say it, just once, do you think? I've waited most of my life to hear it."

There was a look of infinite tenderness in his face. His eyes searched hers reverently.

"I love you," he whispered huskily. "With my heart. With my mind. With my body and my soul. I'd do anything for you."

The tears rolled slowly down her cheeks, and she laughed with delight, triumph, shyness. "Oh, John," she moaned, pressing down hard against him. "Oh, John, I love you so much!"

"How would you like to come into the bedroom and show me how much?" he murmured dryly, but it wasn't completely a joke, because his body was already telling her that he needed more than words.

She bent and kissed his eyes, his nose, the dimple in his chin, and his hard mouth. "Will you let me?" she implored daringly.

His eyes opened, blue fires staring up into hers. "All the way?" he asked softly.

"Yes."

He searched her eyes. "I've never let a woman take me," he said quietly. "Not in all my life. But I suppose being my wife does give you a few privileges, Mrs. Sterling," he mused.

She bent and kissed him softly. "I'll be very gentle with you," she whispered, teasing, but he pulled her mouth down hard, and the kiss he gave her was anything but humorous.

It was the most incredible experience of her life. He lay sprawled on the mattress like a sacrificial victim, letting her make new discoveries about his body and its responses. Letting her touch and taste and stroke him, until he groaned aloud, until his big body trembled. And all through it he smiled and laughed, and his eyes blazed like blue coals while he watched her, guided her, whispered and coaxed and gloried in her fascination, the laziness of his smile at variance with the tension that built to explosive force in him.

When he was just seconds away from losing his mind, he ended the torment himself, whipping her over and crushing her under him, dragging her down with him into a maelstrom unlike anything he'd ever experienced before. It took him a long time to be able to move without shuddering, to speak. Her own plateau had been nearly as high, and she trembled gently in the aftermath.

She smoothed his hair, kissed his flushed face, stroked his chest and arms until he calmed.

"My God," he breathed, opening his eyes at last, and they were filled with wonder as they searched her face.

"I can't believe I really did all that," she said flushing. Her eyes fell to his mouth. "I'd never even read about some of those things."

"It's called instinct," he managed. "When it's coupled with love, it goes a long way. I've never climbed that high before," he added with a slow smile. "I'm having trouble coming back down again, as you see."

She blushed again and slid down against his body, holding him. "Does this help?"

He caught her hips and moved them against his. "This helps more." He eased himself over her body and smiled at the shock in her eyes. "Yes, I know," he laughed. "The books say this is impossible, don't they? Lie still. This time," he breathed as his mouth opened over hers, "is going to blow your mind . . ."

She could hardly stand in the shower later while he soaped her body under the warm spray. She clung to him weakly, and he laughed.

"Worn out already?" he teased. "You'll have to take vitamins."

"You're marvelous," she whispered at his lips. "Worth waiting all my life for."

"I could return that compliment," he murmured, smiling as he kissed her. "No lingering doubts? No second thoughts?"

She shook her head, and her eyes adored him. "I'll take care of you all my life. I'll be the best wife you could ever want."

"You already are," he said. He held her against him warmly, without passion, his head bent over hers. "It won't be easy sometimes. We won't have a lot at first. But I'll work hard to give you the best life I can. And even if we don't have money, Priss, we'll have love. Of the two, that's the more important." He kissed her forehead. "I'll spend the rest of my life making up to you those five years we lost."

"I'll do the same for you," she promised. "Darling, darling, I can hardly believe it's happened! It's like a sweet dream. I'd rather

die than wake up and find it isn't real at all."
Tears stung her eyes. "I've lived on dreams for
so long . . ."

"So have I," he whispered, nuzzling his
face against her damp hair as he held her.
"But we have each other now. Forever,
Priss."

She kissed his chest affectionately. "Later
on, I'll give you a son."

He trembled a little. His hands contracted. "How much later on?" he whispered.

She looked up at him quietly. "Whenever
you like."

He was breathing unsteadily. "I'm thirty-
three already."

"Then . . . we'd better not wait . . . too
long," she whispered at his lips.

"A few months—no more," he whispered
back. "I'd like a baby."

"So would I." She pressed herself completely against him, loving the freedom love gave
her to be so intimate with him. She closed her
eyes. "You're a nice bloke, John Sterling." She
grinned. "Gone to the pack, of course, but . . .
ooh!"

He pinched her and laughed at her expression. "Shut up and wash my back, woman. I
want my tucker."

"Big, bad Australian," she teased. "I can
see right off that you're going to be a horrible
bully."

"Not to you, mate," he murmured and kissed her.

She smiled under his mouth, loving the feel and taste of it. The years ahead were going to be the best of her life; she already knew it. And the best part was loving this big, burly Australian who'd given her his wild heart. Dreams did come true, it seemed. Because she was holding hers in her arms.

An epic novel of exotic rituals
and the lure of the Upper Amazon

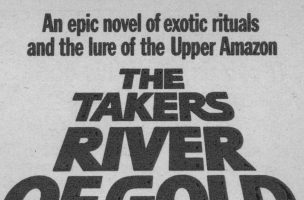

THE TAKERS RIVER OF GOLD

JERRY AND S.A. AHERN

THE TAKERS are the intrepid Josh Culhane and the seductive Mary Mulrooney. These two adventurers launch an incredible journey into the Brazilian rain forest. Far upriver, the jungle yields its deepest secret—the lost city of the Amazon warrior women!

THE TAKERS series is making publishing history. Awarded *The Romantic Times* first prize for High Adventure in 1984, the opening book in the series was hailed by *The Romantic Times* as "the next trend in romance writing and reading. Highly recommended!"

Jerry and S.A. Ahern have never been better!
